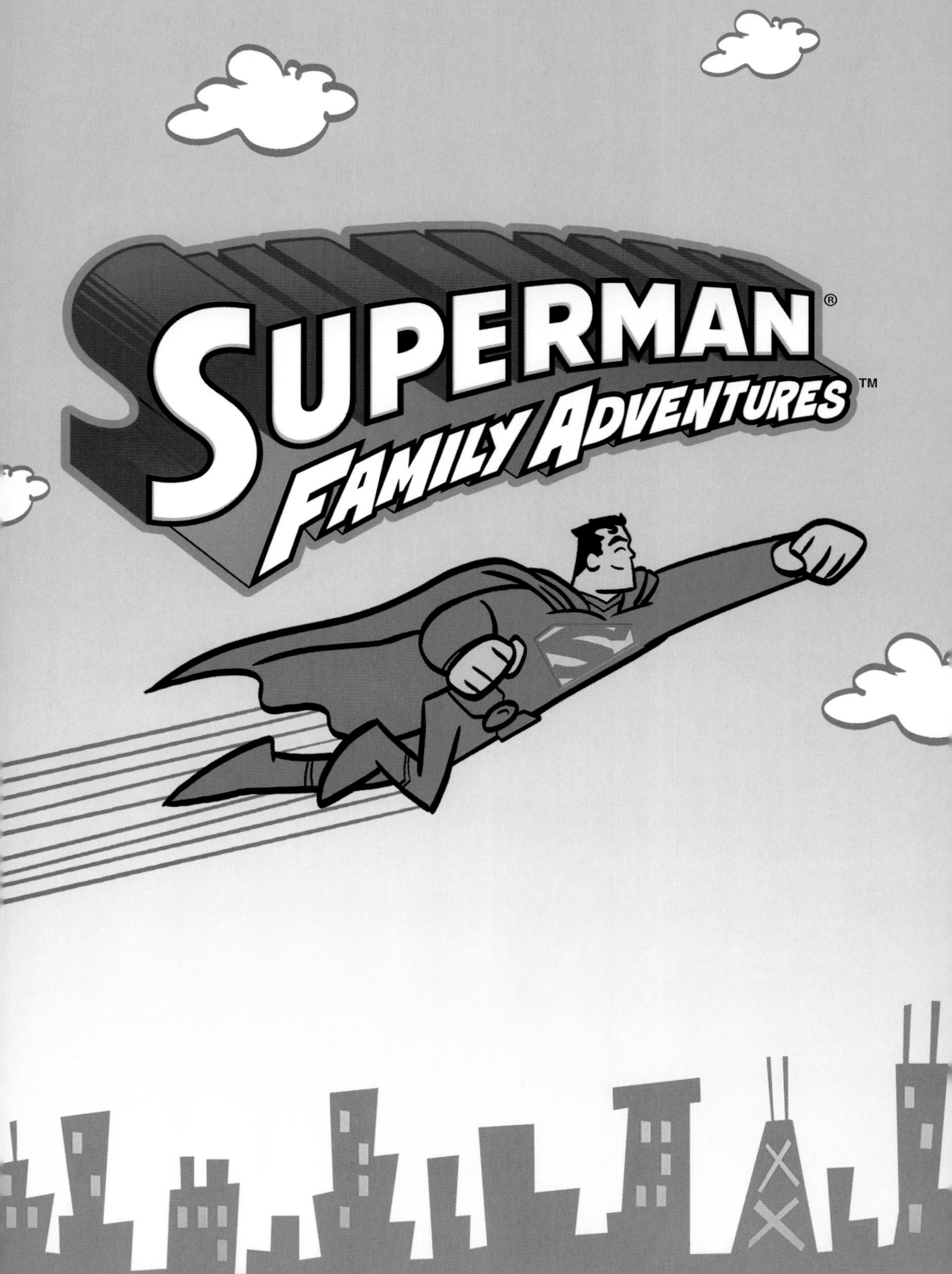
SUPERMAN®
FAMILY ADVENTURES™

STONE ARCH BOOKS
a capstone imprint

STONE ARCH BOOKS™

Published in 2013
A Capstone Imprint
1710 Roe Crest Drive
North Mankato, MN 56003
www.capstonepub.com

Originally published by DC Comics in the U.S. in single
magazine form as SUPERMAN FAMILY ADVENTURES #1.
Copyright © 2013 DC Comics. All Rights Reserved.

DC Comics
1700 Broadway, New York, NY 10019
A Warner Bros. Entertainment Company

Cataloging-in-Publication Data is available at the
Library of Congress website:
ISBN: 978-1-4342-4786-5 (library binding)

Summary: Superman's closest allies take the stage like you have
never seen before! Don't miss the action-packed, history-making,
super adventure awesomeness!! Classic Superman elements
reinterpreted for all ages with the humor that only the creative
team of Tiny Titans can bring!

STONE ARCH BOOKS

Ashley C. Andersen Zantop Publisher
Michael Dahl Editorial Director
Donald Lemke Editor
Brann Garvey Designer
Kathy McColley Production Specialist

DC COMICS

Kristy Quinn Original U.S. Editor

Printed in China by Nordica.
0413/CA21300442
032013 007226NORDF13

SUPERMAN® FAMILY ADVENTURES™

The Adventures Begin!

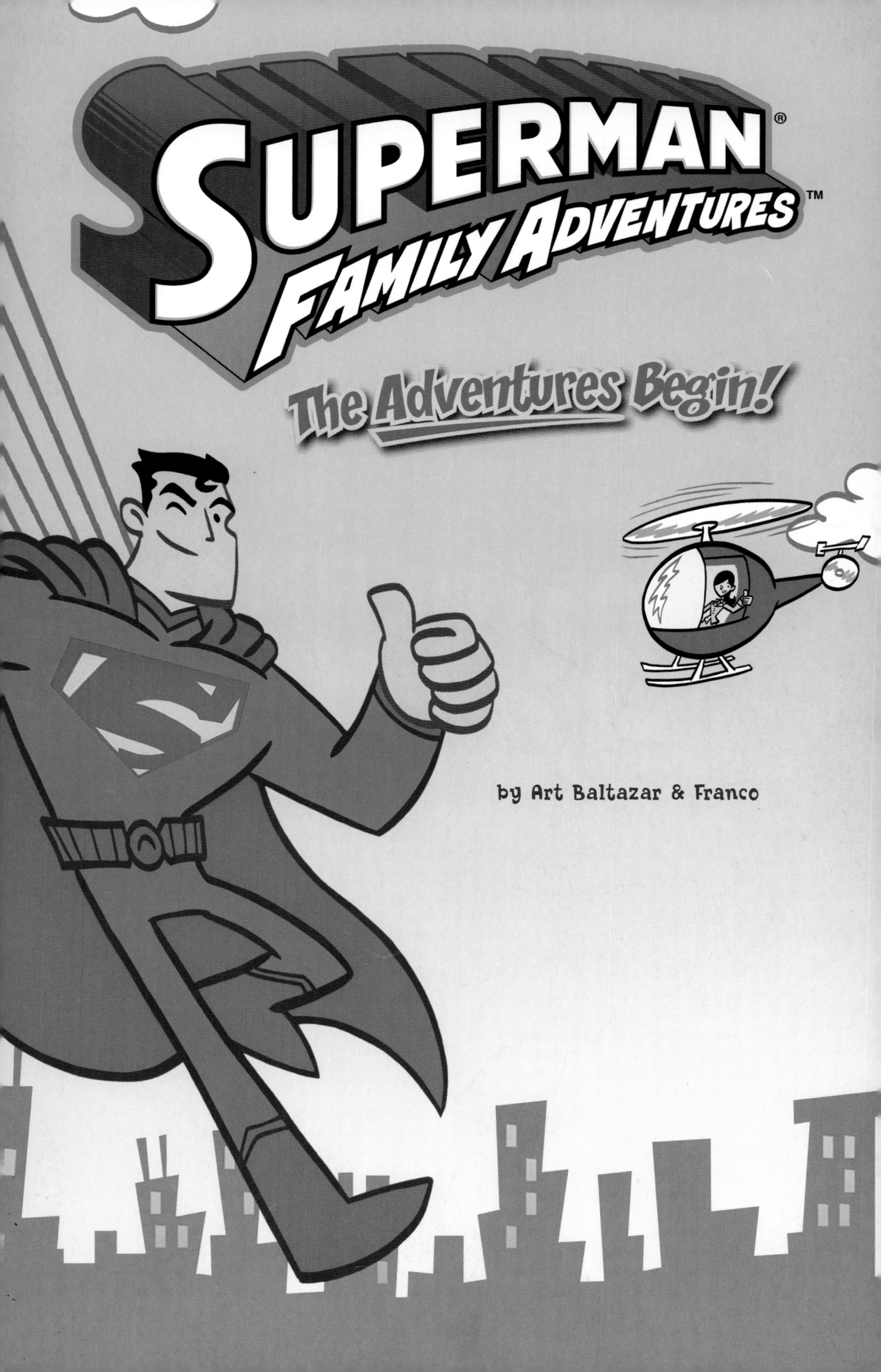

by Art Baltazar & Franco

SUPERMAN® FAMILY ADVENTURES™

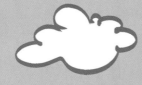

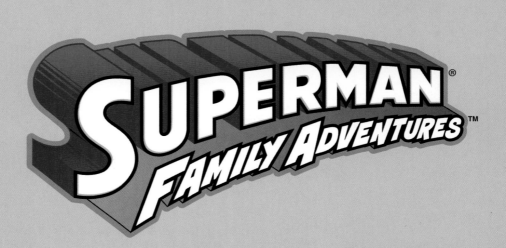

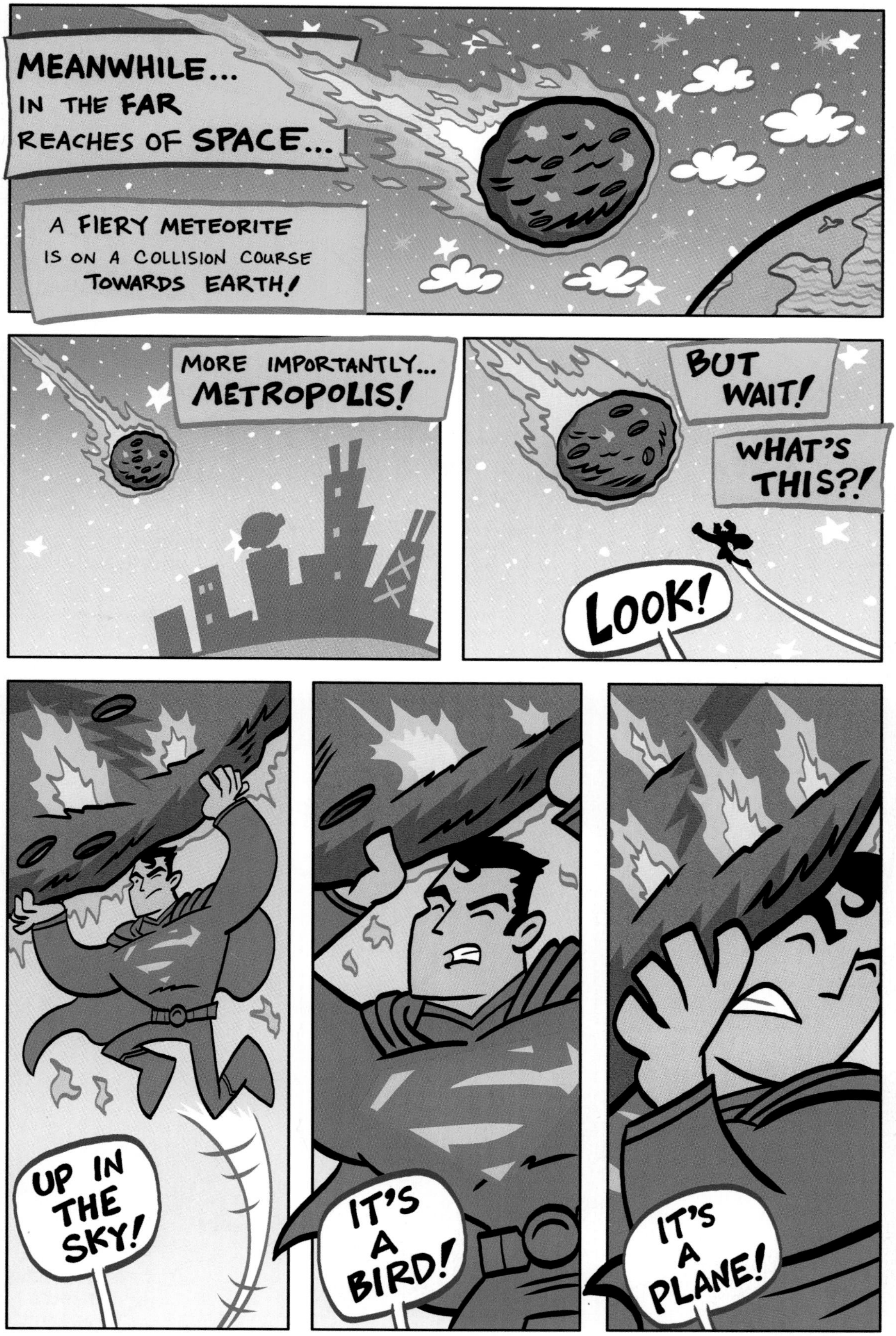
MEANWHILE... IN THE FAR REACHES OF SPACE...
A FIERY METEORITE IS ON A COLLISION COURSE TOWARDS EARTH!
MORE IMPORTANTLY... METROPOLIS!
BUT WAIT!
WHAT'S THIS?!
LOOK!
UP IN THE SKY!
IT'S A BIRD!
IT'S A PLANE!

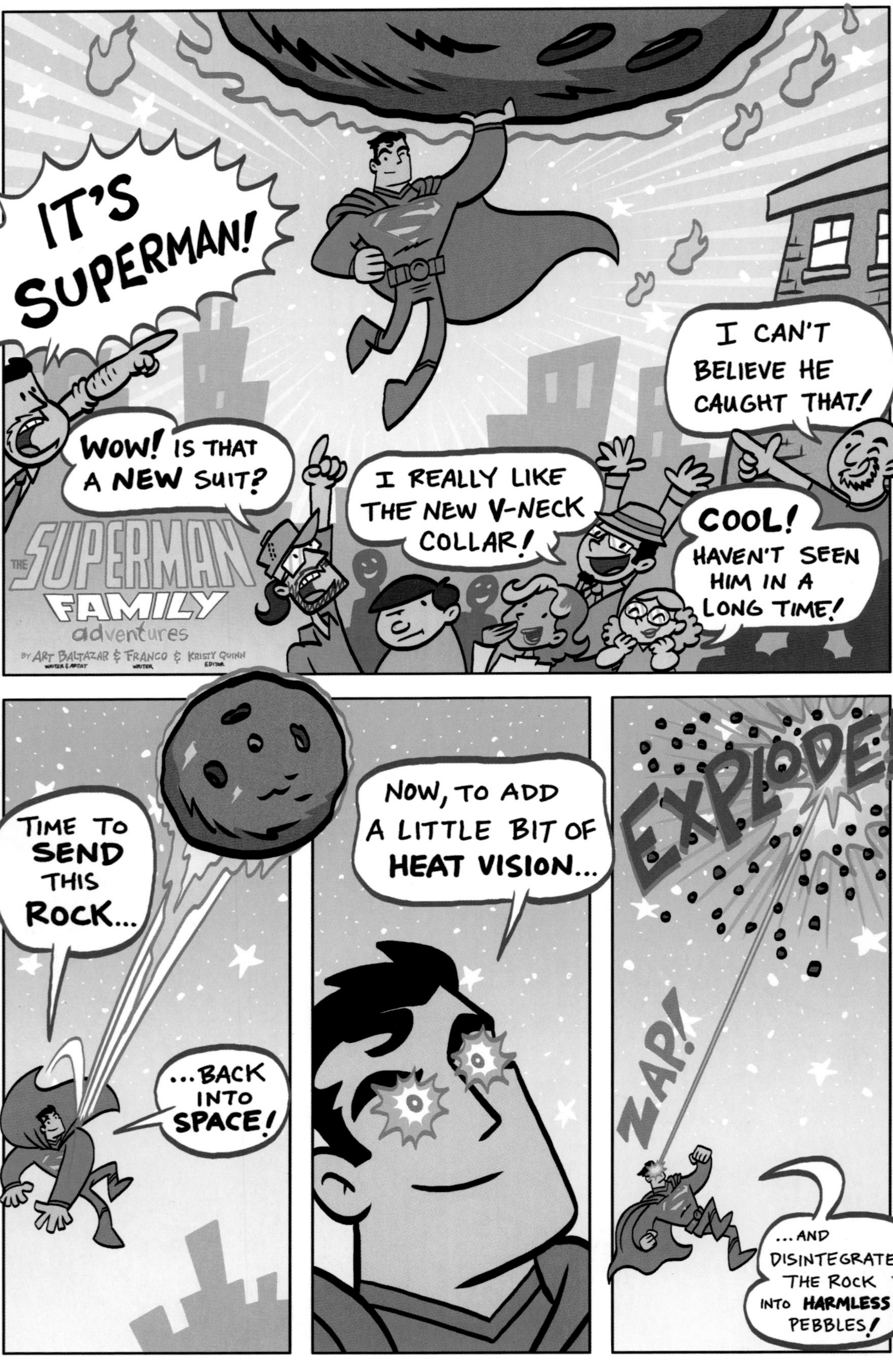
IT'S SUPERMAN!
WOW! IS THAT A NEW SUIT?
I REALLY LIKE THE NEW V-NECK COLLAR!
I CAN'T BELIEVE HE CAUGHT THAT!
COOL! HAVEN'T SEEN HIM IN A LONG TIME!
THE SUPERMAN FAMILY adventures
BY ART BALTAZAR WRITER & ARTIST & FRANCO WRITER & KRISTY QUINN EDITOR
TIME TO SEND THIS ROCK...
...BACK INTO SPACE!
NOW, TO ADD A LITTLE BIT OF HEAT VISION...
EXPLODE!
ZAP!
...AND DISINTEGRATE THE ROCK INTO HARMLESS PEBBLES!

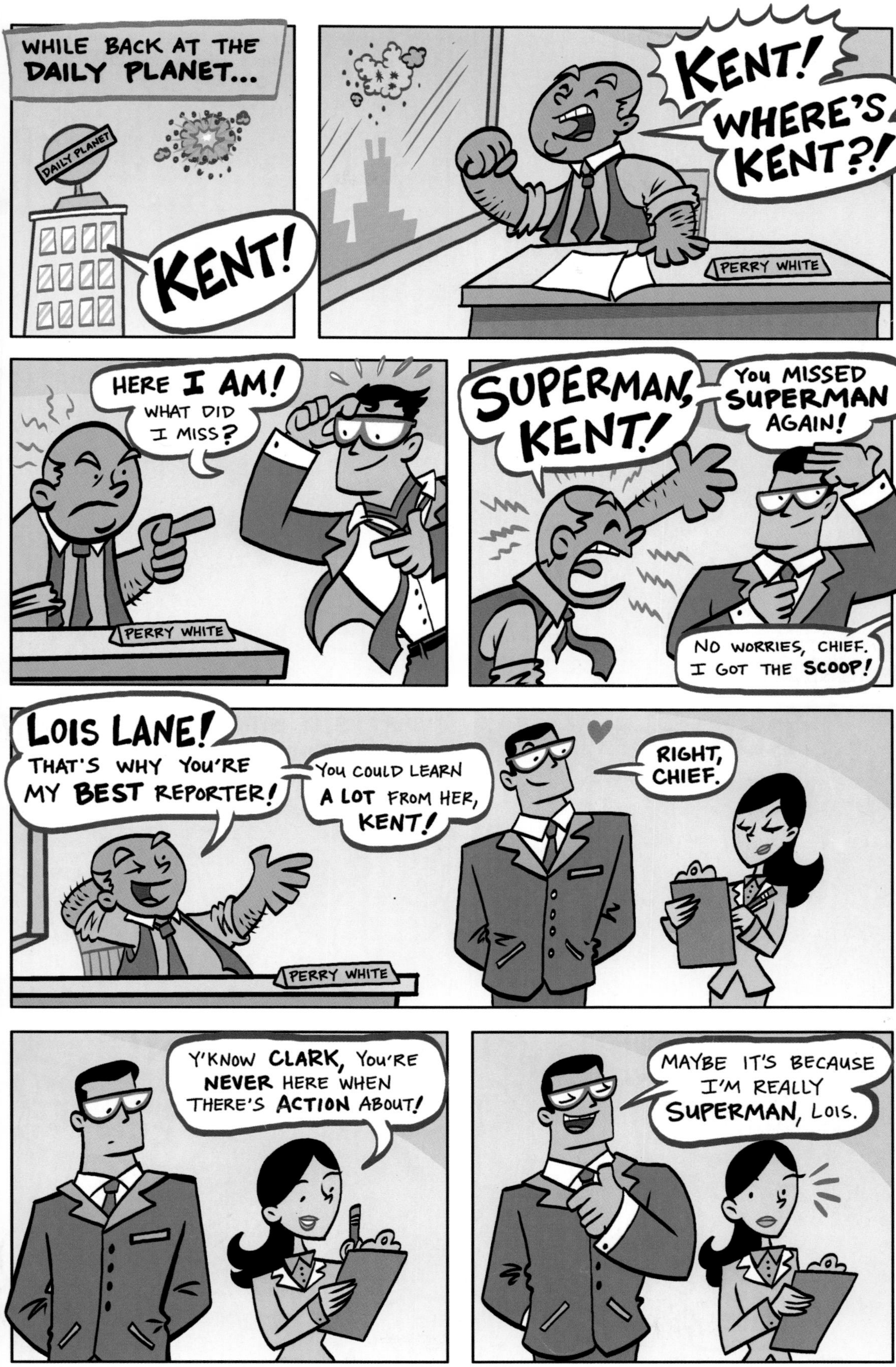
WHILE BACK AT THE DAILY PLANET...
DAILY PLANET
KENT!
KENT! WHERE'S KENT?!
PERRY WHITE
HERE I AM! WHAT DID I MISS?
PERRY WHITE
SUPERMAN, KENT!
YOU MISSED SUPERMAN AGAIN!
NO WORRIES, CHIEF. I GOT THE SCOOP!
LOIS LANE! THAT'S WHY YOU'RE MY BEST REPORTER!
YOU COULD LEARN A LOT FROM HER, KENT!
RIGHT, CHIEF.
PERRY WHITE
Y'KNOW CLARK, YOU'RE NEVER HERE WHEN THERE'S ACTION ABOUT!
MAYBE IT'S BECAUSE I'M REALLY SUPERMAN, LOIS.

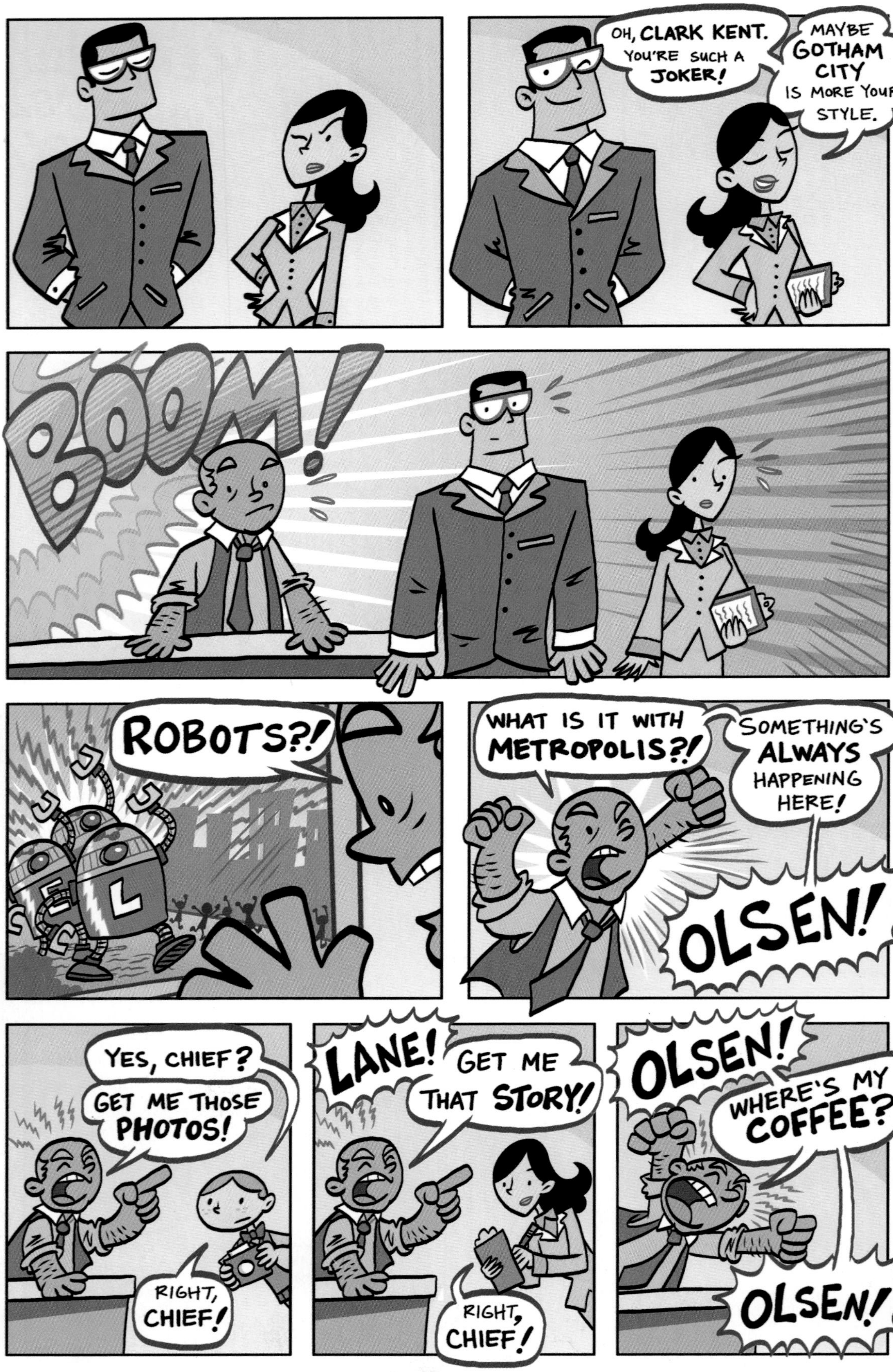
OH, CLARK KENT. YOU'RE SUCH A JOKER!
MAYBE GOTHAM CITY IS MORE YOUR STYLE.
BOOM!
ROBOTS?!
WHAT IS IT WITH METROPOLIS?!
SOMETHING'S ALWAYS HAPPENING HERE!
OLSEN!
YES, CHIEF?
GET ME THOSE PHOTOS!
RIGHT, CHIEF!
LANE!
GET ME THAT STORY!
RIGHT, CHIEF!
OLSEN!
WHERE'S MY COFFEE?
OLSEN!

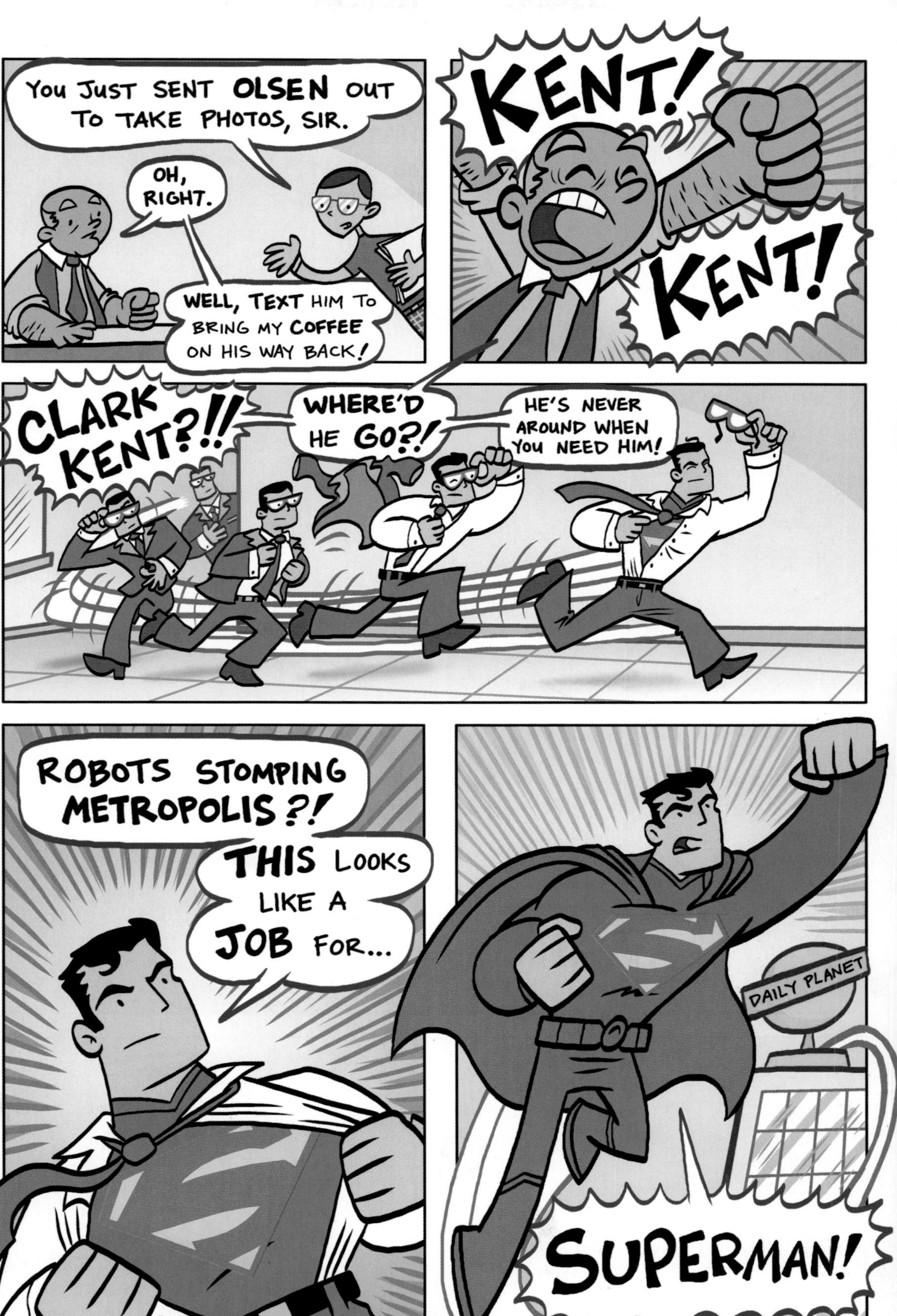
YOU JUST SENT OLSEN OUT TO TAKE PHOTOS, SIR.
OH, RIGHT.
WELL, TEXT HIM TO BRING MY COFFEE ON HIS WAY BACK!
KENT!
KENT!
CLARK KENT?!!
WHERE'D HE GO?!
HE'S NEVER AROUND WHEN YOU NEED HIM!
ROBOTS STOMPING METROPOLIS?!
THIS LOOKS LIKE A JOB FOR...
DAILY PLANET
SUPERMAN!

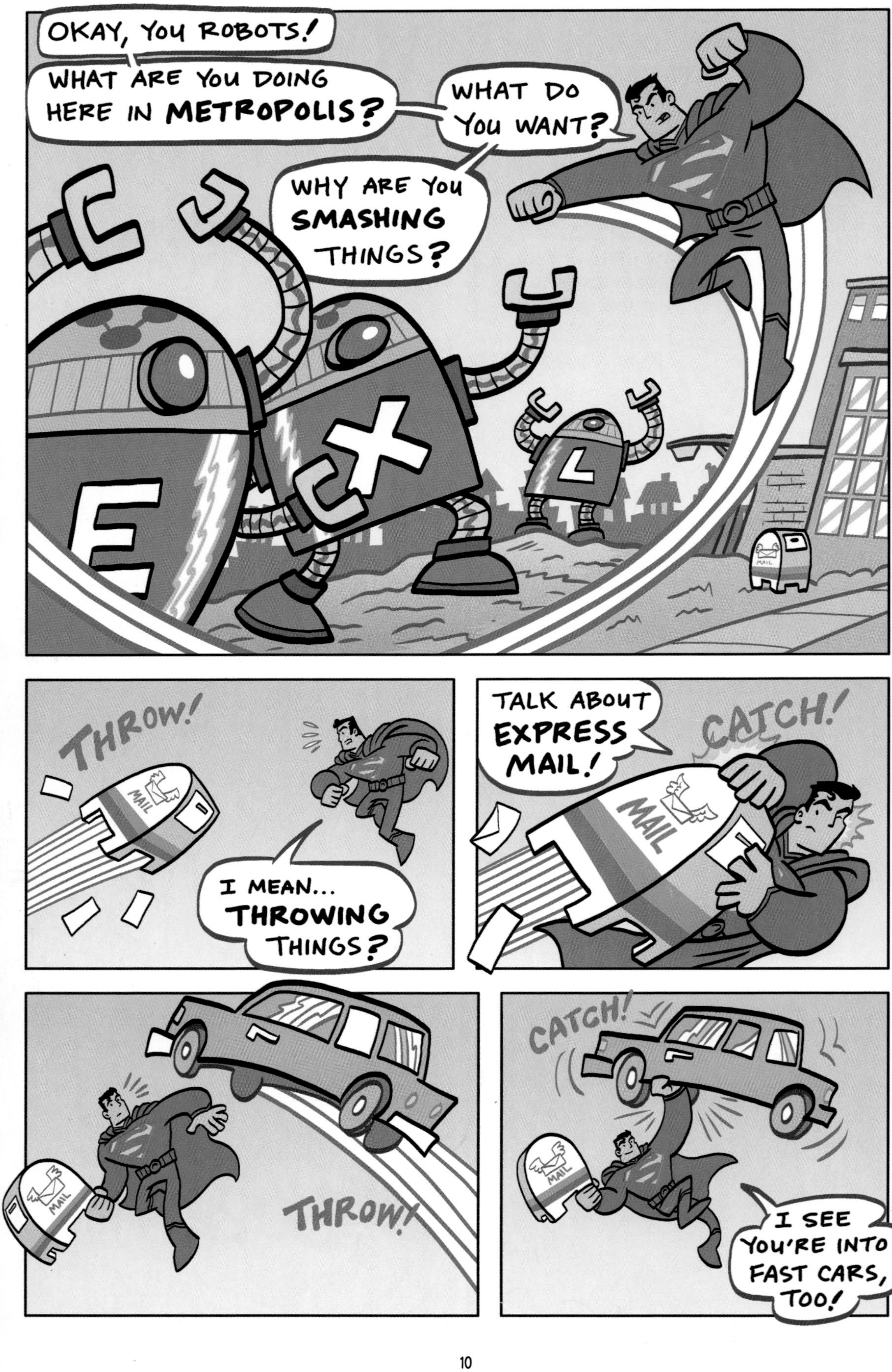
OKAY, YOU ROBOTS!
WHAT ARE YOU DOING HERE IN METROPOLIS?
WHAT DO YOU WANT?
WHY ARE YOU SMASHING THINGS?
E
X
L
MAIL
THROW!
MAIL
I MEAN... THROWING THINGS?
TALK ABOUT EXPRESS MAIL!
CATCH!
MAIL
MAIL
THROW!
CATCH!
MAIL
I SEE YOU'RE INTO FAST CARS, TOO!

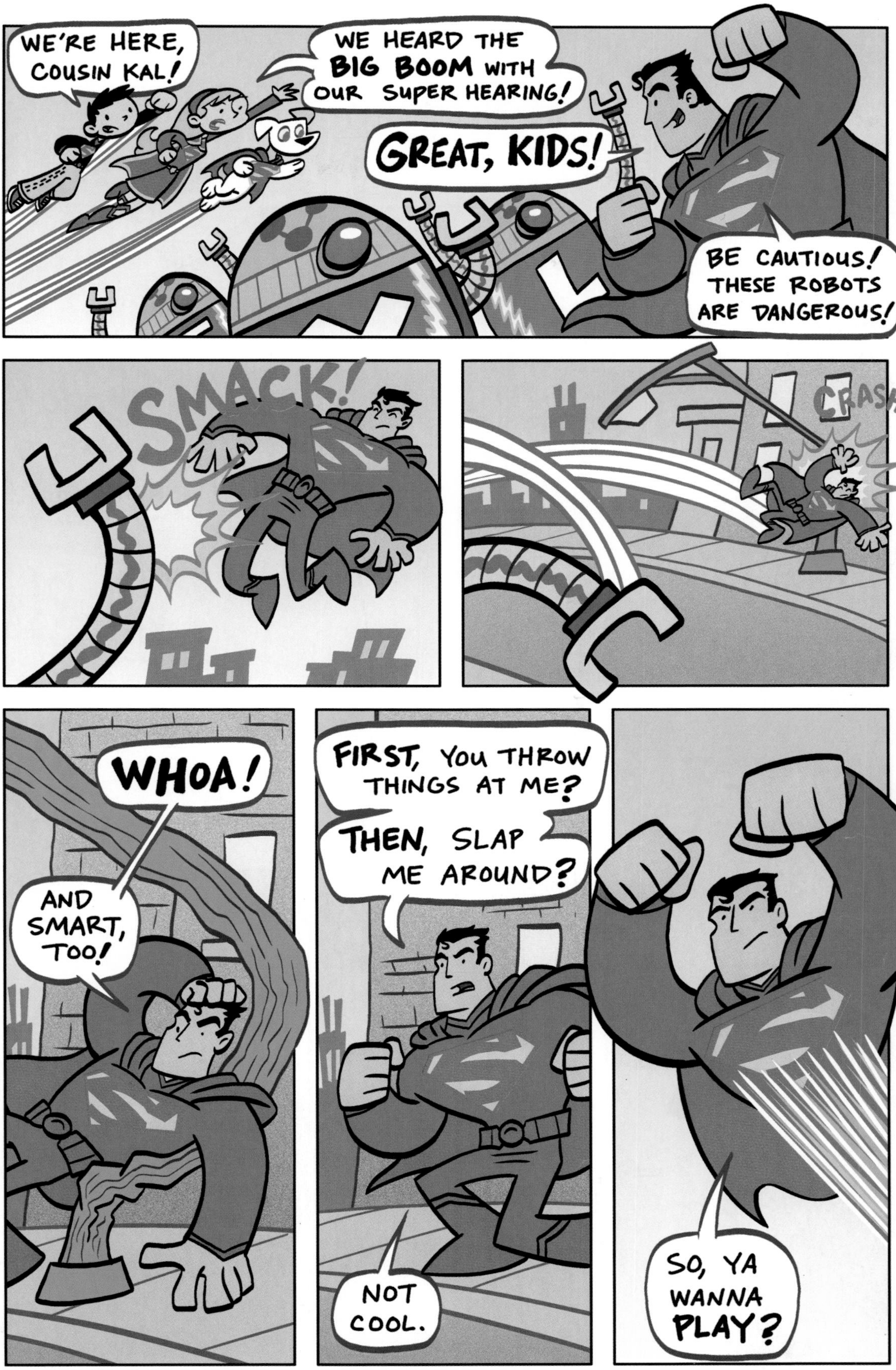
WE'RE HERE, COUSIN KAL!
WE HEARD THE BIG BOOM WITH OUR SUPER HEARING!
GREAT, KIDS!
BE CAUTIOUS! THESE ROBOTS ARE DANGEROUS!
SMACK!
CRASH!
WHOA!
AND SMART, TOO!
FIRST, YOU THROW THINGS AT ME?
THEN, SLAP ME AROUND?
NOT COOL.
SO, YA WANNA PLAY?

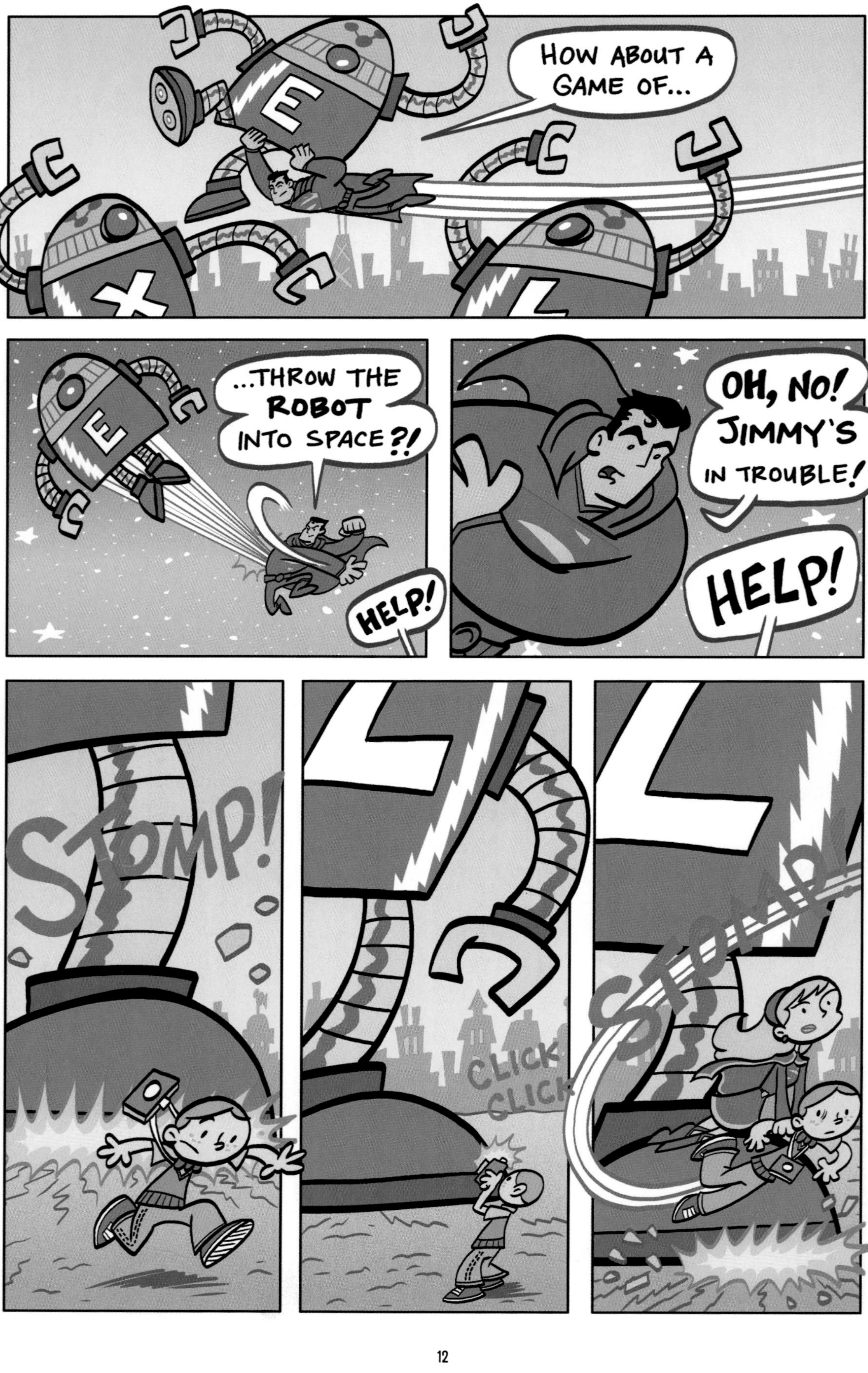
HOW ABOUT A GAME OF...
...THROW THE ROBOT INTO SPACE?!
HELP!
OH, NO! JIMMY'S IN TROUBLE!
HELP!
STOMP!
CLICK CLICK
STOMP!

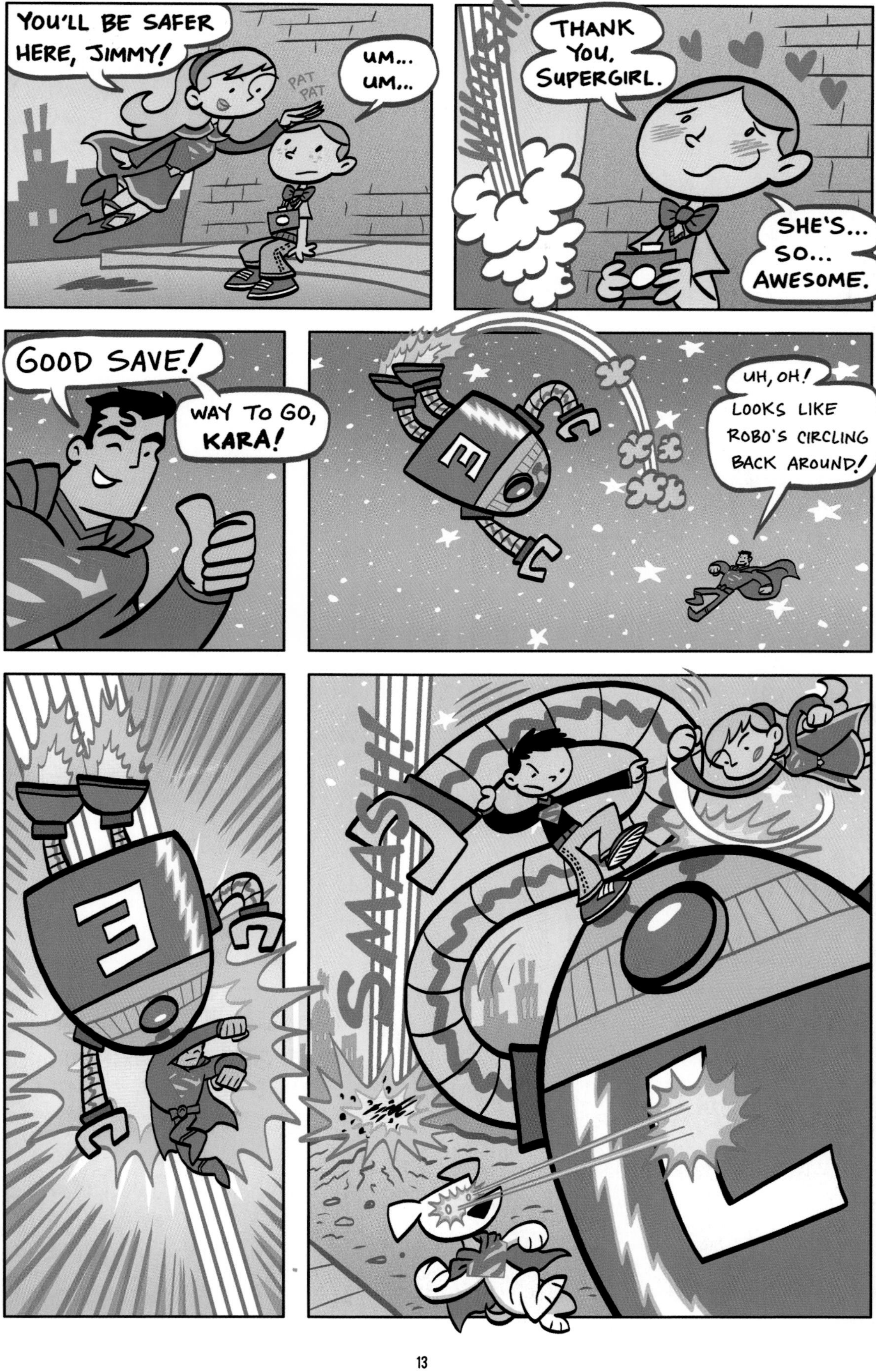
YOU'LL BE SAFER HERE, JIMMY!
PAT PAT
UM... UM...
WHOOSH!
THANK YOU, SUPERGIRL.
SHE'S... SO... AWESOME.
GOOD SAVE!
WAY TO GO, KARA!
UH, OH!
LOOKS LIKE ROBO'S CIRCLING BACK AROUND!
SMASH!

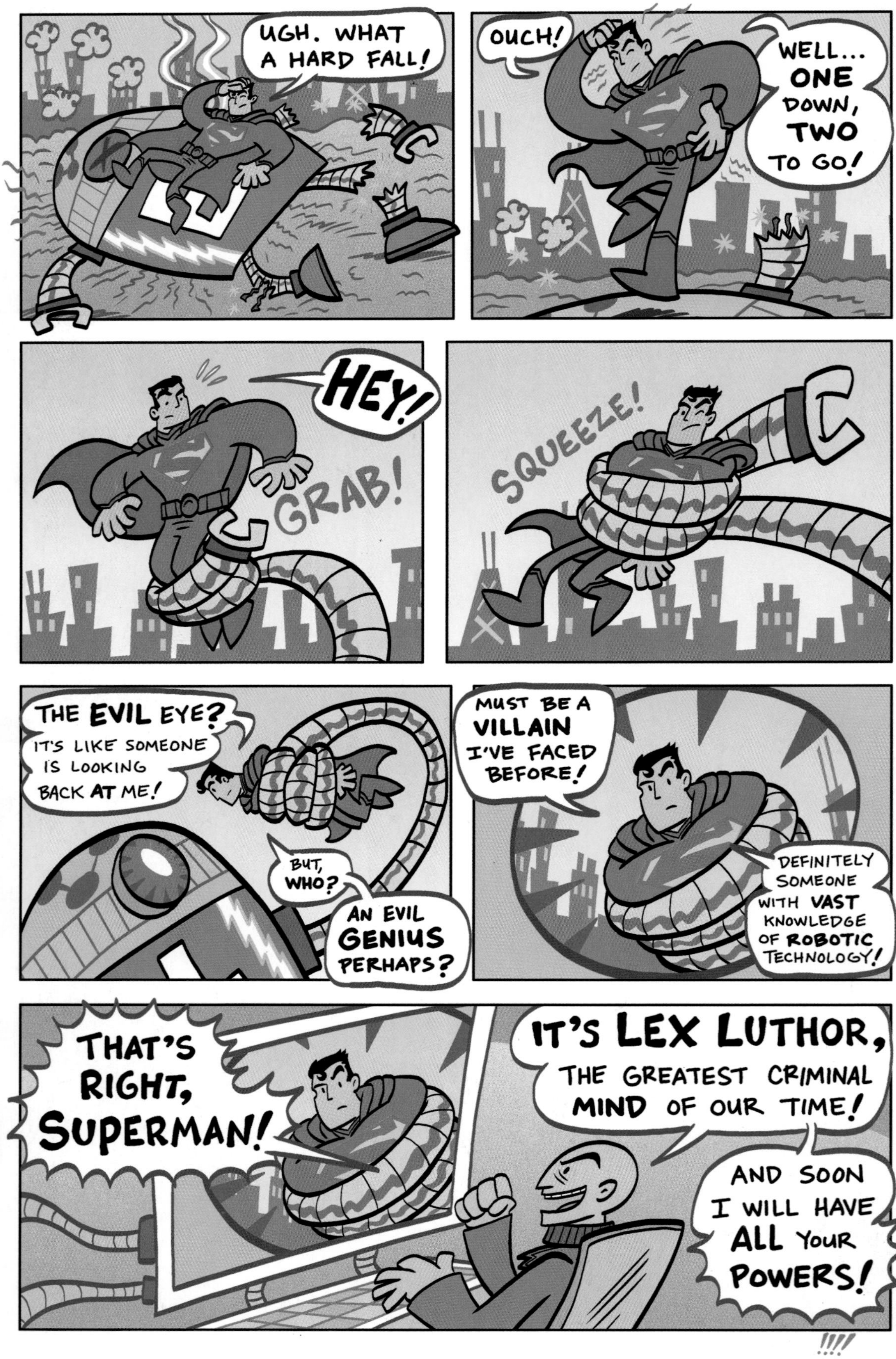
UGH. WHAT A HARD FALL!
OUCH!
WELL... ONE DOWN, TWO TO GO!
HEY!
GRAB!
SQUEEZE!
THE EVIL EYE? IT'S LIKE SOMEONE IS LOOKING BACK AT ME!
BUT, WHO?
AN EVIL GENIUS PERHAPS?
MUST BE A VILLAIN I'VE FACED BEFORE!
DEFINITELY SOMEONE WITH VAST KNOWLEDGE OF ROBOTIC TECHNOLOGY!
THAT'S RIGHT, SUPERMAN!
IT'S LEX LUTHOR, THE GREATEST CRIMINAL MIND OF OUR TIME!
AND SOON I WILL HAVE ALL YOUR POWERS!
!!!!

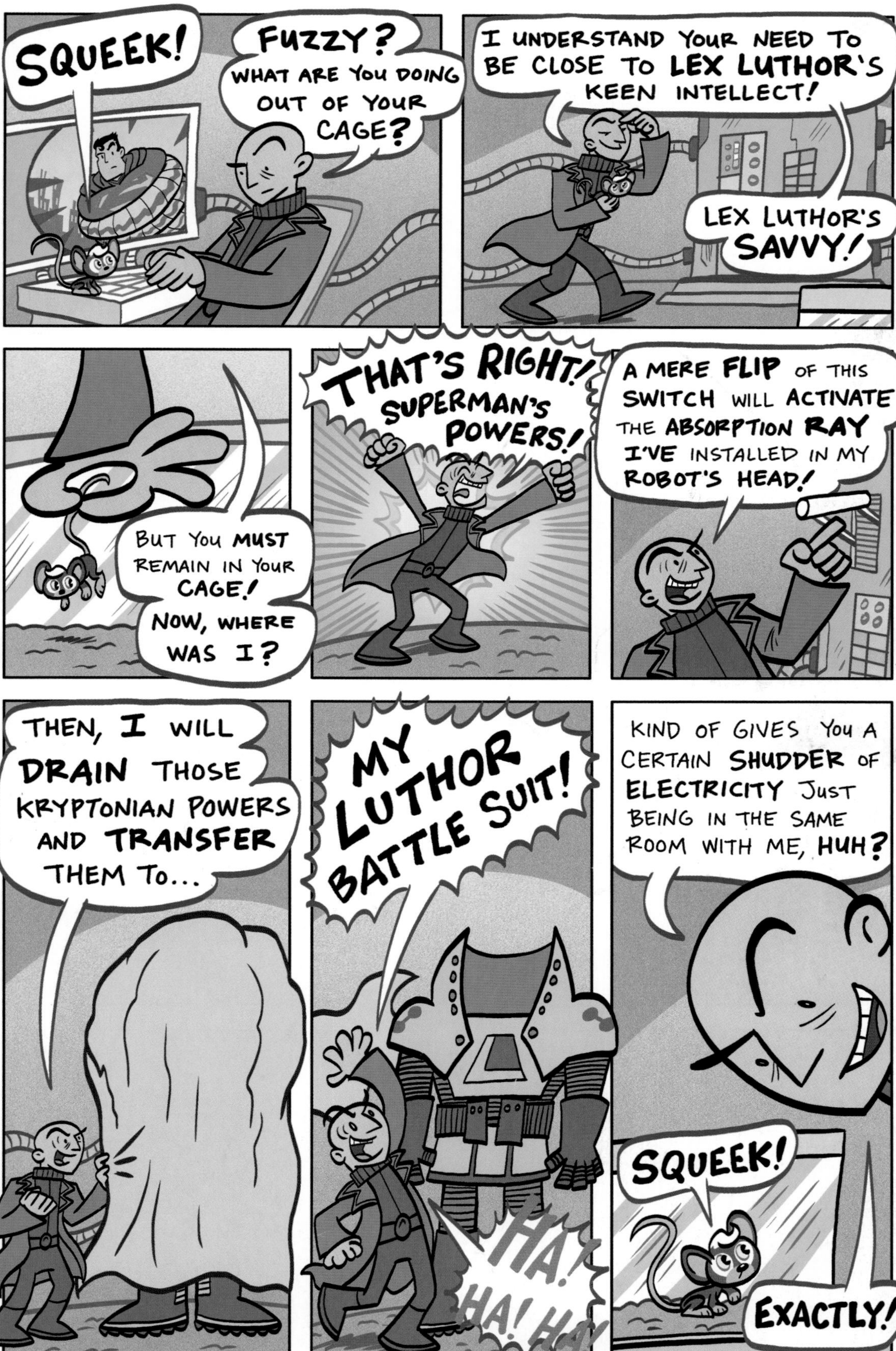
SQUEEK!
FUZZY? WHAT ARE YOU DOING OUT OF YOUR CAGE?
I UNDERSTAND YOUR NEED TO BE CLOSE TO LEX LUTHOR'S KEEN INTELLECT!
LEX LUTHOR'S SAVVY!
BUT YOU MUST REMAIN IN YOUR CAGE!
NOW, WHERE WAS I?
THAT'S RIGHT! SUPERMAN'S POWERS!
A MERE FLIP OF THIS SWITCH WILL ACTIVATE THE ABSORPTION RAY I'VE INSTALLED IN MY ROBOT'S HEAD!
THEN, I WILL DRAIN THOSE KRYPTONIAN POWERS AND TRANSFER THEM TO...
MY LUTHOR BATTLE SUIT!
HA! HA! HA!
KIND OF GIVES YOU A CERTAIN SHUDDER OF ELECTRICITY JUST BEING IN THE SAME ROOM WITH ME, HUH?
SQUEEK!
EXACTLY!

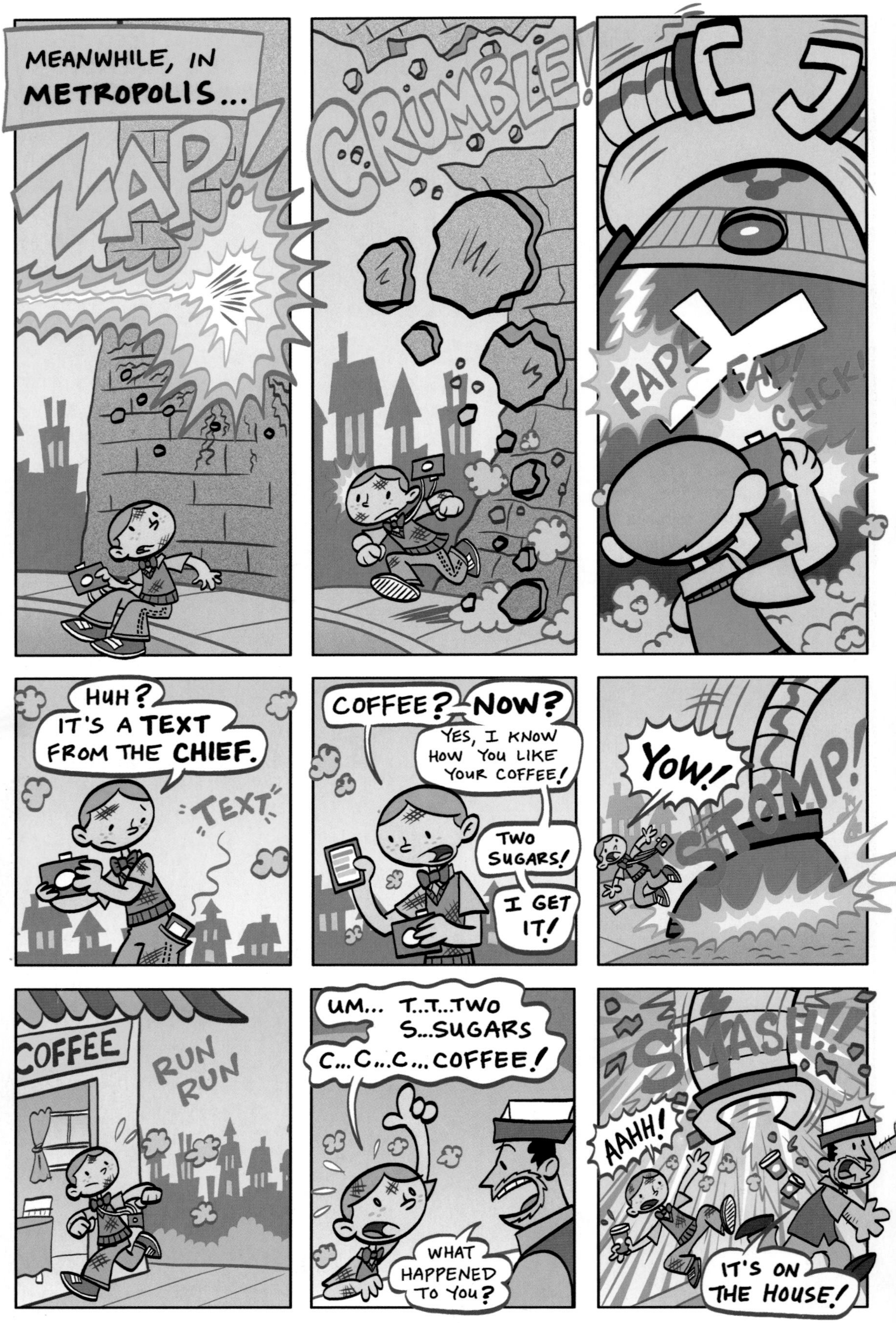
MEANWHILE, IN METROPOLIS...
ZAP!
CRUMBLE!
FAP! FAP! CLICK!
HUH? IT'S A TEXT FROM THE CHIEF.
TEXT
COFFEE?
NOW?
YES, I KNOW HOW YOU LIKE YOUR COFFEE!
TWO SUGARS!
I GET IT!
YOW!
STOMP!
COFFEE
RUN RUN
UM... T...T...TWO S...SUGARS C...C...C... COFFEE!
WHAT HAPPENED TO YOU?
SMASH!!
AAHH!
IT'S ON THE HOUSE!

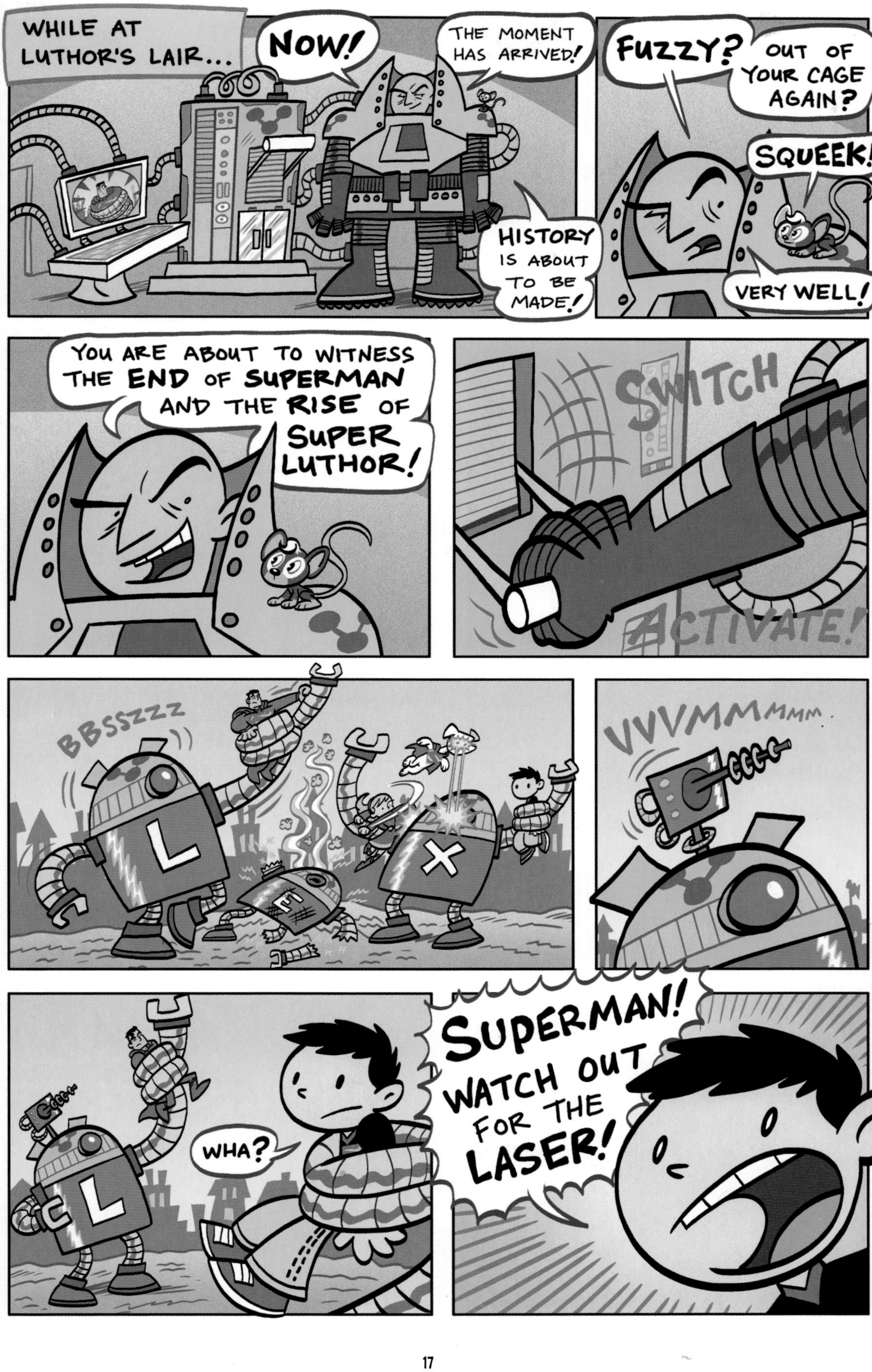
WHILE AT LUTHOR'S LAIR...
NOW!
THE MOMENT HAS ARRIVED!
HISTORY IS ABOUT TO BE MADE!
FUZZY? OUT OF YOUR CAGE AGAIN?
SQUEEK!
VERY WELL!
YOU ARE ABOUT TO WITNESS THE END OF SUPERMAN AND THE RISE OF SUPER LUTHOR!
SWITCH ACTIVATE!
BBSZZZ
VVVMMMMMM
WHA?
SUPERMAN! WATCH OUT FOR THE LASER!

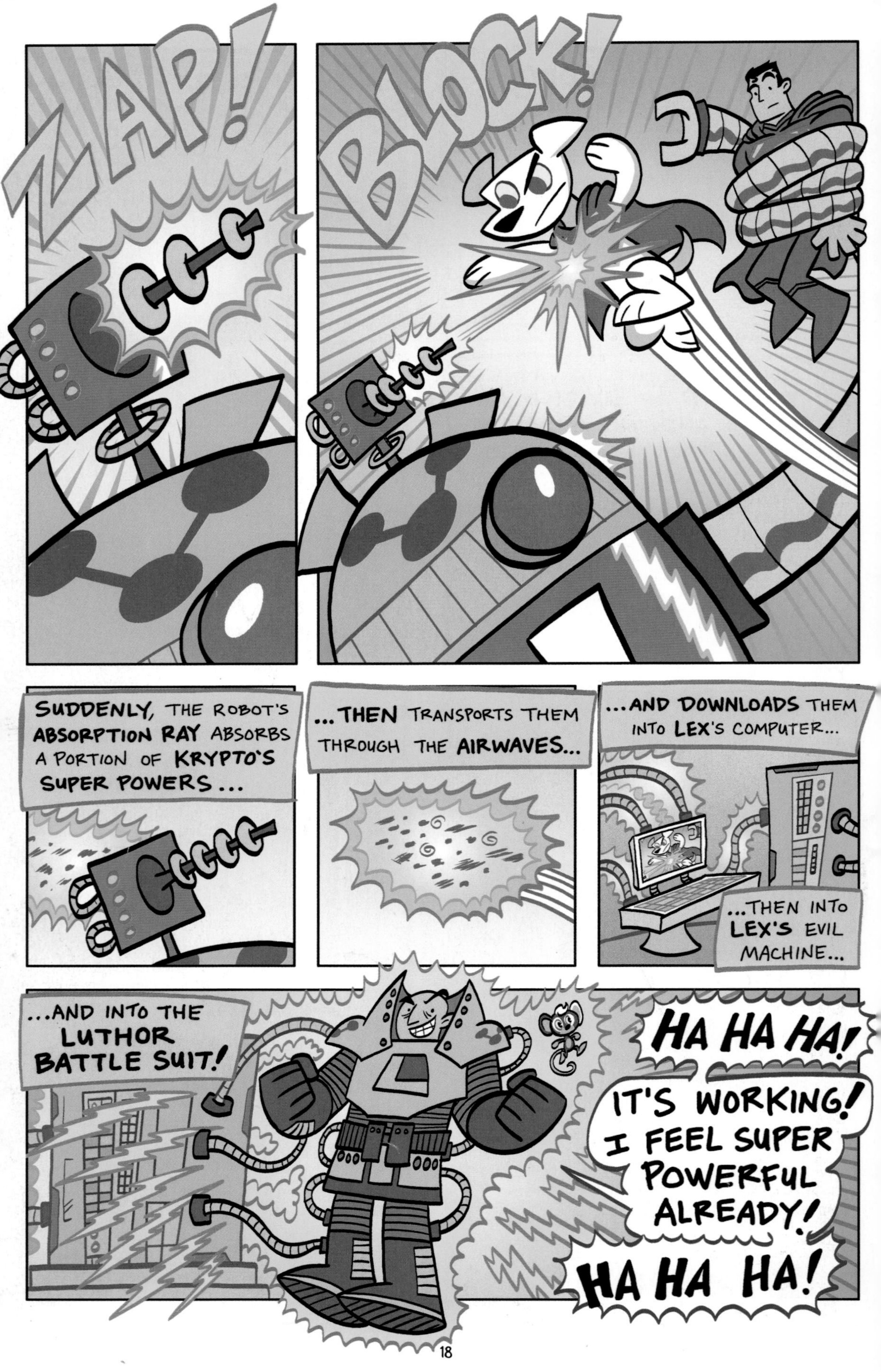
ZAP!
BLOCK!
SUDDENLY, THE ROBOT'S ABSORPTION RAY ABSORBS A PORTION OF KRYPTO'S SUPER POWERS...
...THEN TRANSPORTS THEM THROUGH THE AIRWAVES...
...AND DOWNLOADS THEM INTO LEX'S COMPUTER...
...THEN INTO LEX'S EVIL MACHINE...
...AND INTO THE LUTHOR BATTLE SUIT!
HA HA HA!
IT'S WORKING! I FEEL SUPER POWERFUL ALREADY!
HA HA HA!

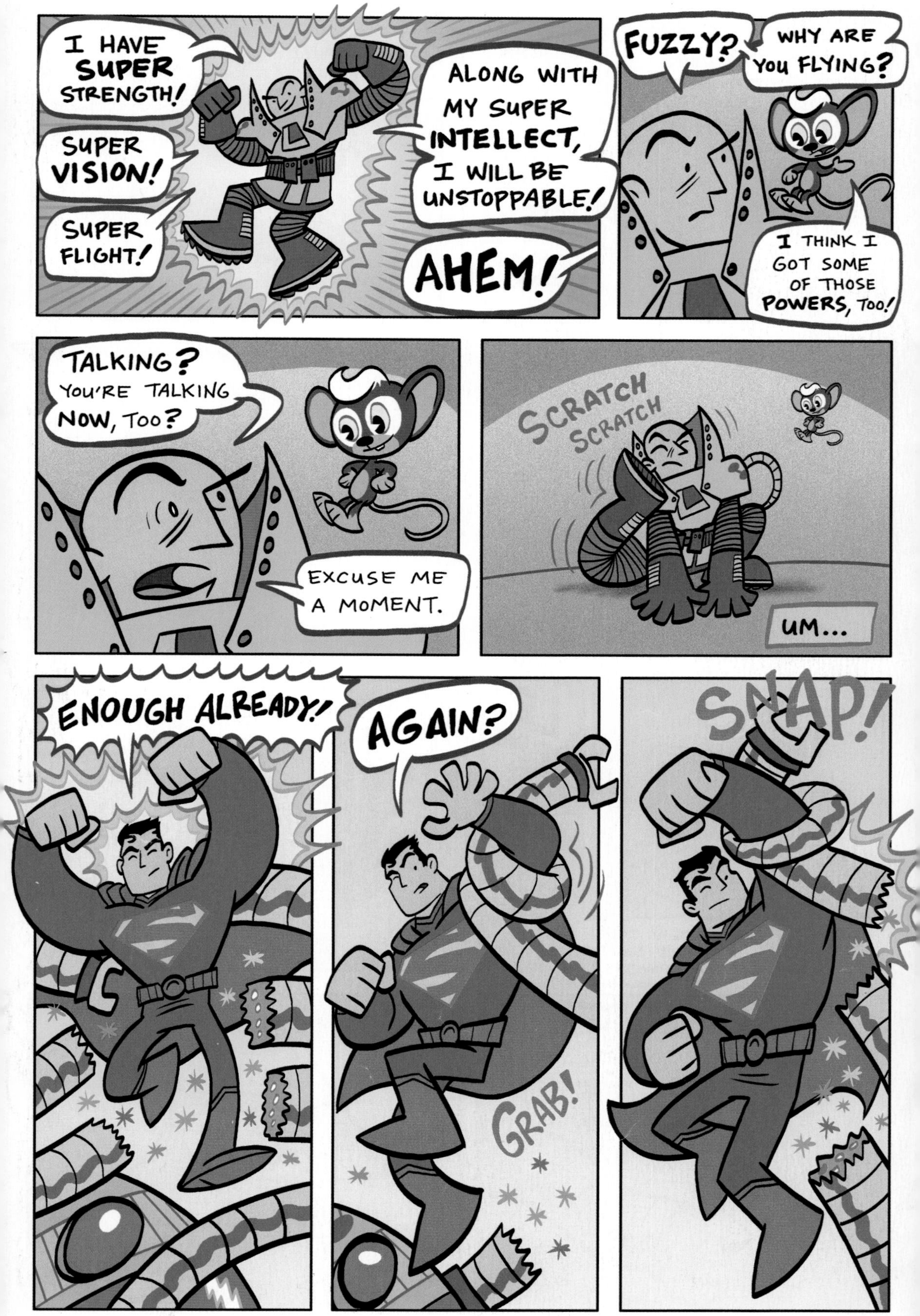
I HAVE SUPER STRENGTH!
SUPER VISION!
SUPER FLIGHT!
ALONG WITH MY SUPER INTELLECT, I WILL BE UNSTOPPABLE!
AHEM!
FUZZY?
WHY ARE YOU FLYING?
I THINK I GOT SOME OF THOSE POWERS, TOO!
TALKING? YOU'RE TALKING NOW, TOO?
EXCUSE ME A MOMENT.
SCRATCH
SCRATCH
UM...
ENOUGH ALREADY!
AGAIN?
GRAB!
SNAP!

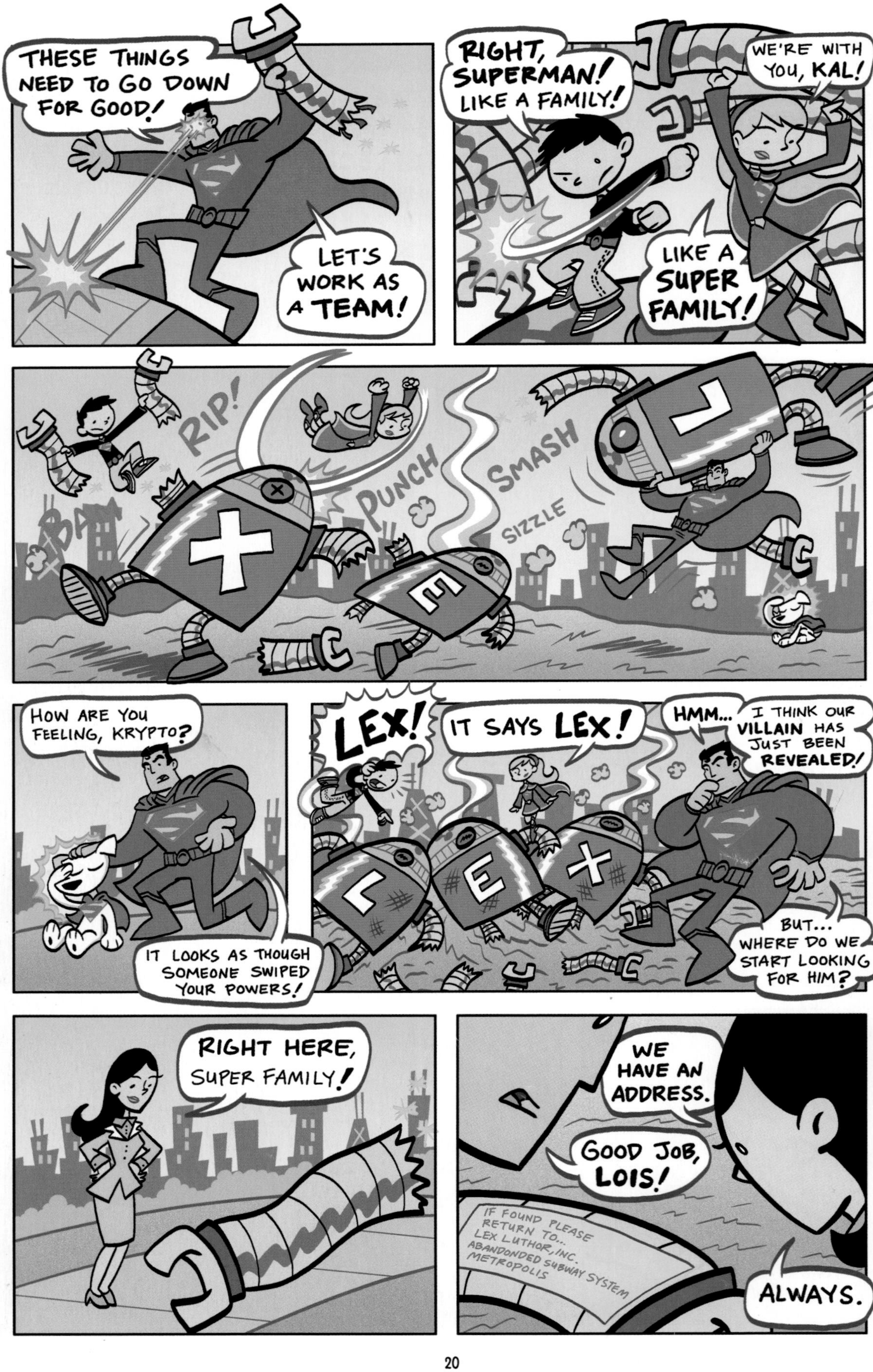
THESE THINGS NEED TO GO DOWN FOR GOOD!
LET'S WORK AS A TEAM!
RIGHT, SUPERMAN! LIKE A FAMILY!
WE'RE WITH YOU, KAL!
LIKE A SUPER FAMILY!
RIP!
PUNCH
SMASH
SIZZLE
HOW ARE YOU FEELING, KRYPTO?
IT LOOKS AS THOUGH SOMEONE SWIPED YOUR POWERS!
LEX!
IT SAYS LEX!
HMM...
I THINK OUR VILLAIN HAS JUST BEEN REVEALED!
BUT... WHERE DO WE START LOOKING FOR HIM?
RIGHT HERE, SUPER FAMILY!
WE HAVE AN ADDRESS.
GOOD JOB, LOIS!
IF FOUND PLEASE RETURN TO... LEX LUTHOR, INC. ABANDONED SUBWAY SYSTEM METROPOLIS
ALWAYS.

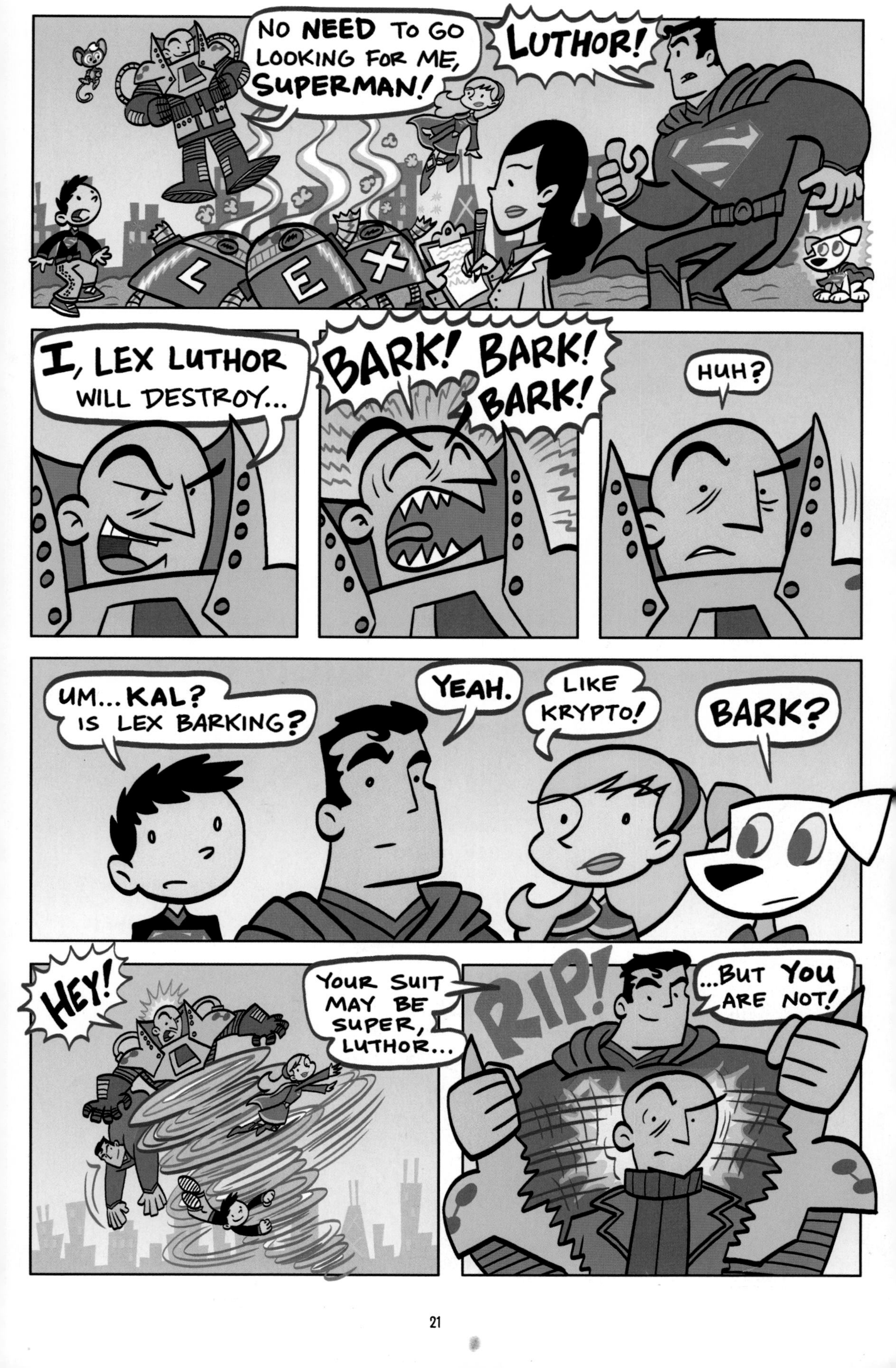
NO NEED TO GO LOOKING FOR ME, SUPERMAN!
LUTHOR!
L E X
I, LEX LUTHOR WILL DESTROY...
BARK! BARK! BARK!
HUH?
UM...KAL? IS LEX BARKING?
YEAH.
LIKE KRYPTO!
BARK?
HEY!
YOUR SUIT MAY BE SUPER, LUTHOR...
RIP!
...BUT YOU ARE NOT!

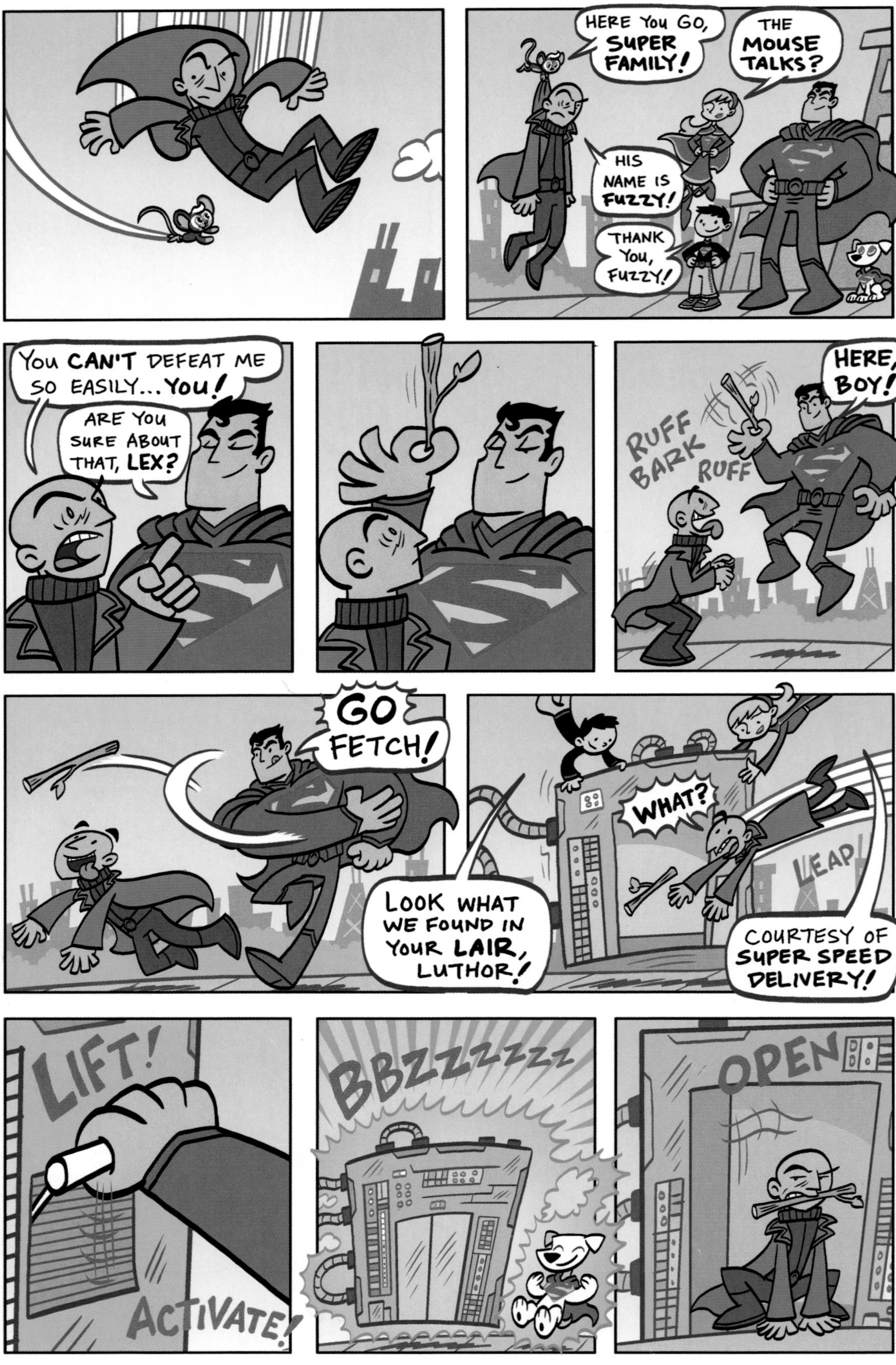
HERE YOU GO, SUPER FAMILY!
THE MOUSE TALKS?
HIS NAME IS FUZZY!
THANK YOU, FUZZY!
YOU CAN'T DEFEAT ME SO EASILY... YOU!
ARE YOU SURE ABOUT THAT, LEX?
HERE, BOY!
RUFF
BARK
RUFF
GO FETCH!
WHAT?
LEAP
LOOK WHAT WE FOUND IN YOUR LAIR, LUTHOR!
COURTESY OF SUPER SPEED DELIVERY!
LIFT!
ACTIVATE!
BBZZZZZZZ
OPEN

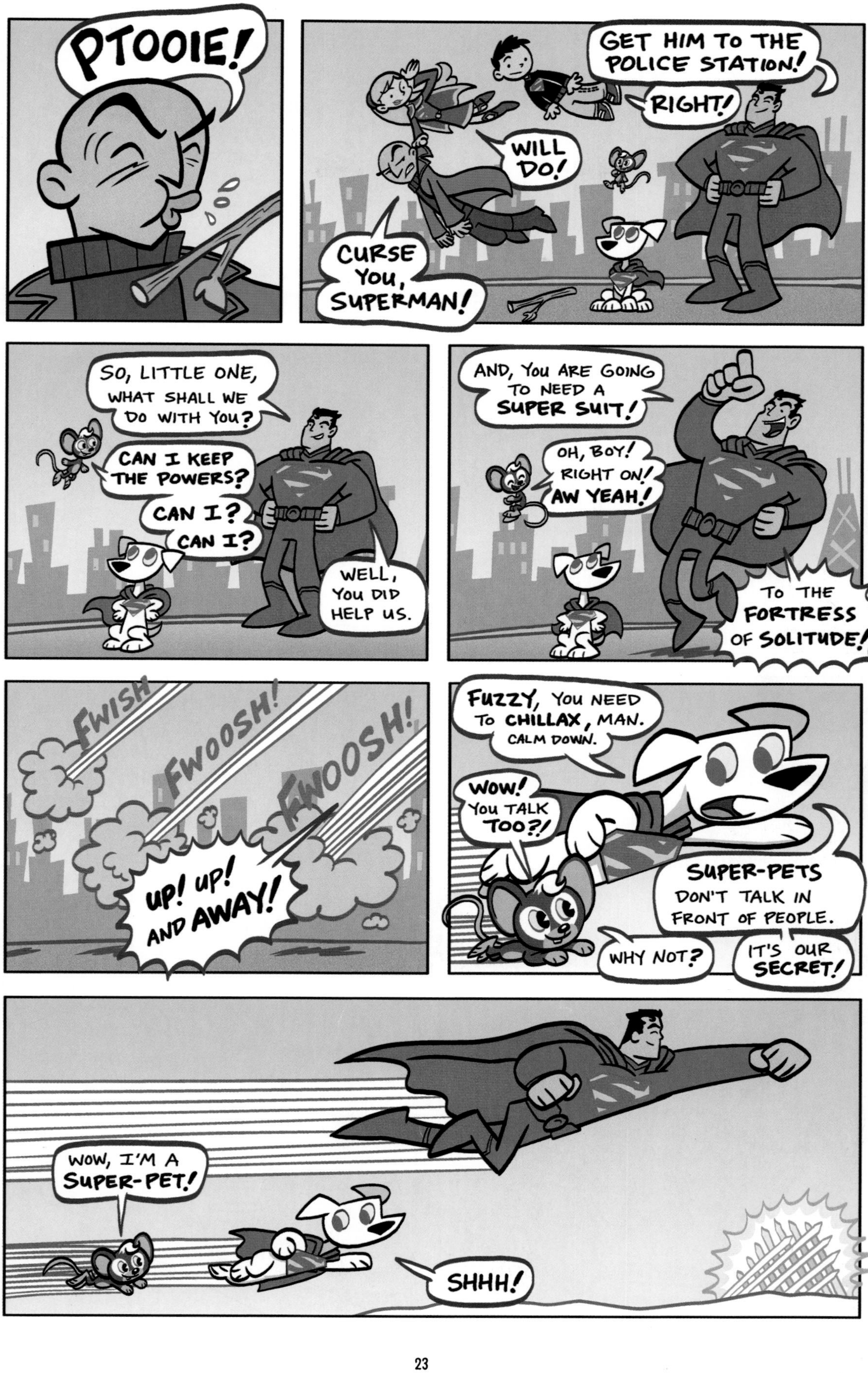
PTOOIE!
GET HIM TO THE POLICE STATION!
RIGHT!
WILL DO!
CURSE YOU, SUPERMAN!
SO, LITTLE ONE, WHAT SHALL WE DO WITH YOU?
CAN I KEEP THE POWERS?
CAN I? CAN I?
WELL, YOU DID HELP US.
AND, YOU ARE GOING TO NEED A SUPER SUIT!
OH, BOY! RIGHT ON! AW YEAH!
TO THE FORTRESS OF SOLITUDE!
FWISH
FWOOSH!
FWOOSH!
UP! UP! AND AWAY!
FUZZY, YOU NEED TO CHILLAX, MAN. CALM DOWN.
WOW! YOU TALK TOO?!
SUPER-PETS DON'T TALK IN FRONT OF PEOPLE.
WHY NOT?
IT'S OUR SECRET!
WOW, I'M A SUPER-PET!
SHHH!

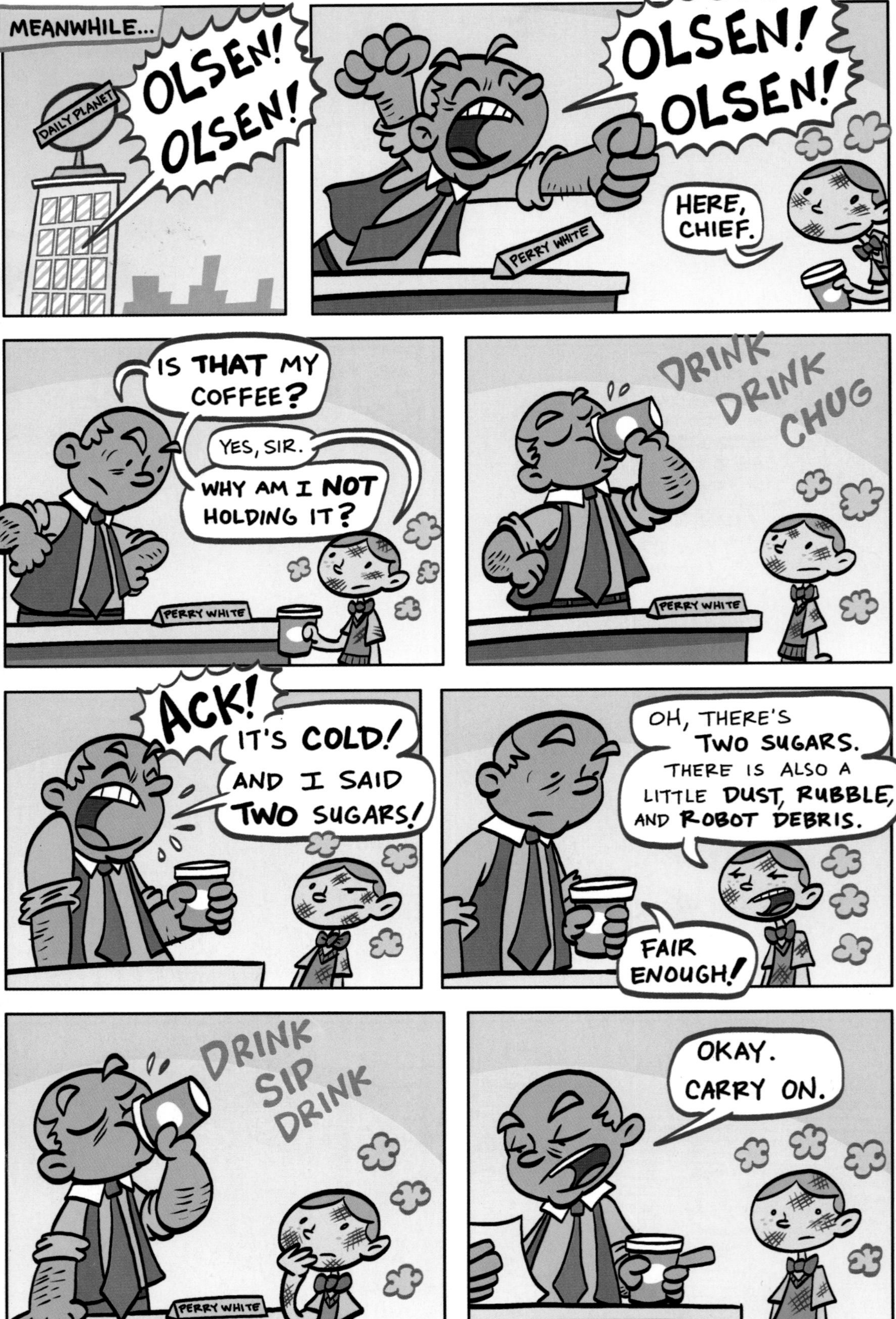
MEANWHILE...
DAILY PLANET
OLSEN! OLSEN!
OLSEN! OLSEN!
PERRY WHITE
HERE, CHIEF.
IS THAT MY COFFEE?
YES, SIR.
WHY AM I NOT HOLDING IT?
PERRY WHITE
DRINK DRINK CHUG
PERRY WHITE
ACK!
IT'S COLD! AND I SAID TWO SUGARS!
OH, THERE'S TWO SUGARS. THERE IS ALSO A LITTLE DUST, RUBBLE, AND ROBOT DEBRIS.
FAIR ENOUGH!
DRINK SIP DRINK
PERRY WHITE
OKAY. CARRY ON.

–DIGGIN' SOME COFFEE, TOO!

SUPERMAN®
FAMILY ADVENTURES™

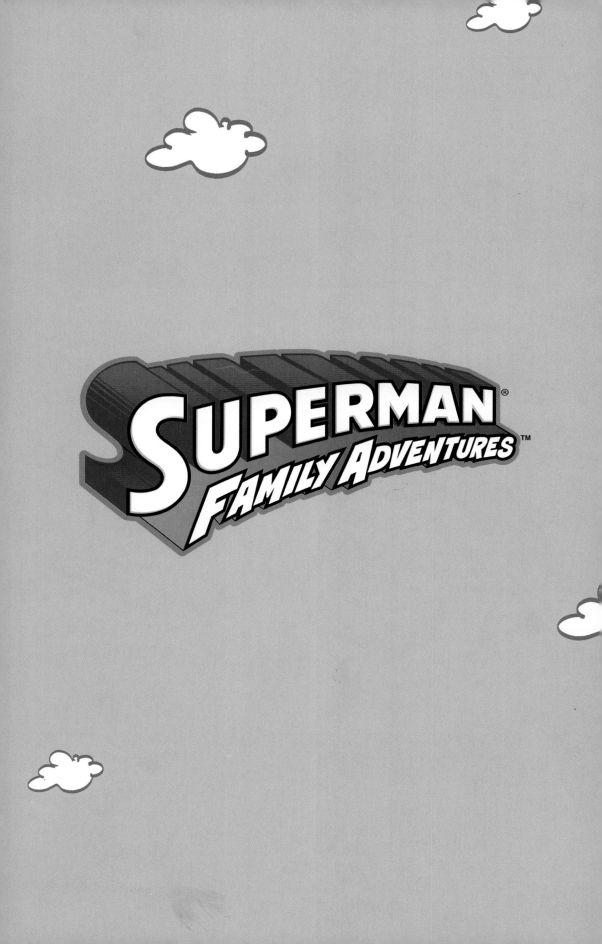

CREATORS

ART BALTAZAR IS A CARTOONIST MACHINE FROM THE HEART OF CHICAGO! HE DEFINES CARTOONS AND COMICS NOT ONLY AS AN ART STYLE, BUT AS A WAY OF LIFE. CURRENTLY, ART IS THE CREATIVE FORCE BEHIND THE NEW YORK TIMES BEST-SELLING, EISNER AWARD-WINNING, DC COMICS SERIES TINY TITANS, AND THE CO-WRITER FOR BILLY BATSON AND THE MAGIC OF SHAZAM! AND CO-CREATOR OF SUPERMAN FAMILY ADVENTURES. ART IS LIVING THE DREAM! HE DRAWS COMICS AND NEVER HAS TO LEAVE THE HOUSE. HE LIVES WITH HIS LOVELY WIFE, ROSE, BIG BOY SONNY, LITTLE BOY GORDON, AND LITTLE GIRL AUDREY. RIGHT ON!

ART BALTAZAR

FRANCO

FRANCO AURELIANI, BRONX, NEW YORK BORN WRITER AND ARTIST, HAS BEEN DRAWING COMICS SINCE HE COULD HOLD A CRAYON. CURRENTLY RESIDING IN UPSTATE NEW YORK WITH HIS WIFE, IVETTE, AND SON, NICOLAS, FRANCO SPENDS MOST OF HIS DAYS IN A BATCAVE-LIKE STUDIO WHERE HE PRODUCES DC'S TINY TITANS COMICS. IN 1995, FRANCO FOUNDED BLINDWOLF STUDIOS, AN INDEPENDENT ART STUDIO WHERE HE AND FELLOW CREATORS CAN CREATE CHILDREN'S COMICS. FRANCO IS THE CREATOR, ARTIST, AND WRITER OF WEIRDSVILLE, L'IL CREEPS, AND EAGLE ALL STAR, AS WELL AS THE CO-CREATOR AND WRITER OF PATRICK THE WOLF BOY. WHEN HE'S NOT WRITING AND DRAWING, FRANCO ALSO TEACHES HIGH SCHOOL ART.

GLOSSARY

absorption (ab-ZORP-shuhn)—the process of soaking up liquid, heat, or light

debris (duh-BREE)—the scattered pieces of something that has been broken or destroyed

disintegrate (diss-IN-tuh-grate)—to break up into small pieces

fiery (FYE-uh-ree)—hot or glowing like a fire

genius (JEEN-yuhss)—an unusually smart or talented person

intellect (IN-tuhl-ekt)—the power of the mind to think, reason, understand, and learn

lair (LAIR)—a hideaway, or a protective shelter

meteorite (MEE-tee-ur-rite)—a remaining part of a meteor that falls to Earth before it has burned up

savvy (SAV-ee)—showing quick practical cleverness

scoop (SKOOP)—a story reported in a newspaper before other papers have a chance to report it

vast (VAST)—huge in area or extent

villain (VIL-uhn)—a wicked or evil person

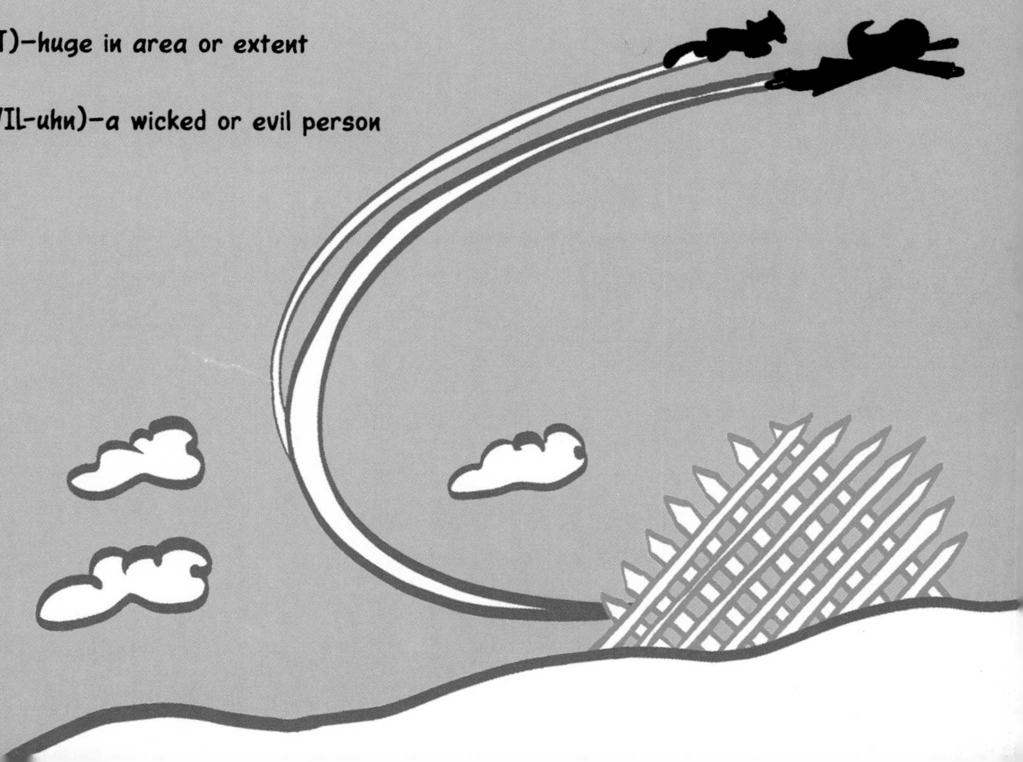

VISUAL QUESTIONS & PROMPTS

1. THE RAMPAGING ROBOTS BELONG TO LEX LUTHOR. WHAT CLUES IN THE ILLUSTRATIONS SUGGEST THAT LEX IS THEIR OWNER? USE EXAMPLES FROM THE STORY TO SUPPORT YOUR ANSWER.

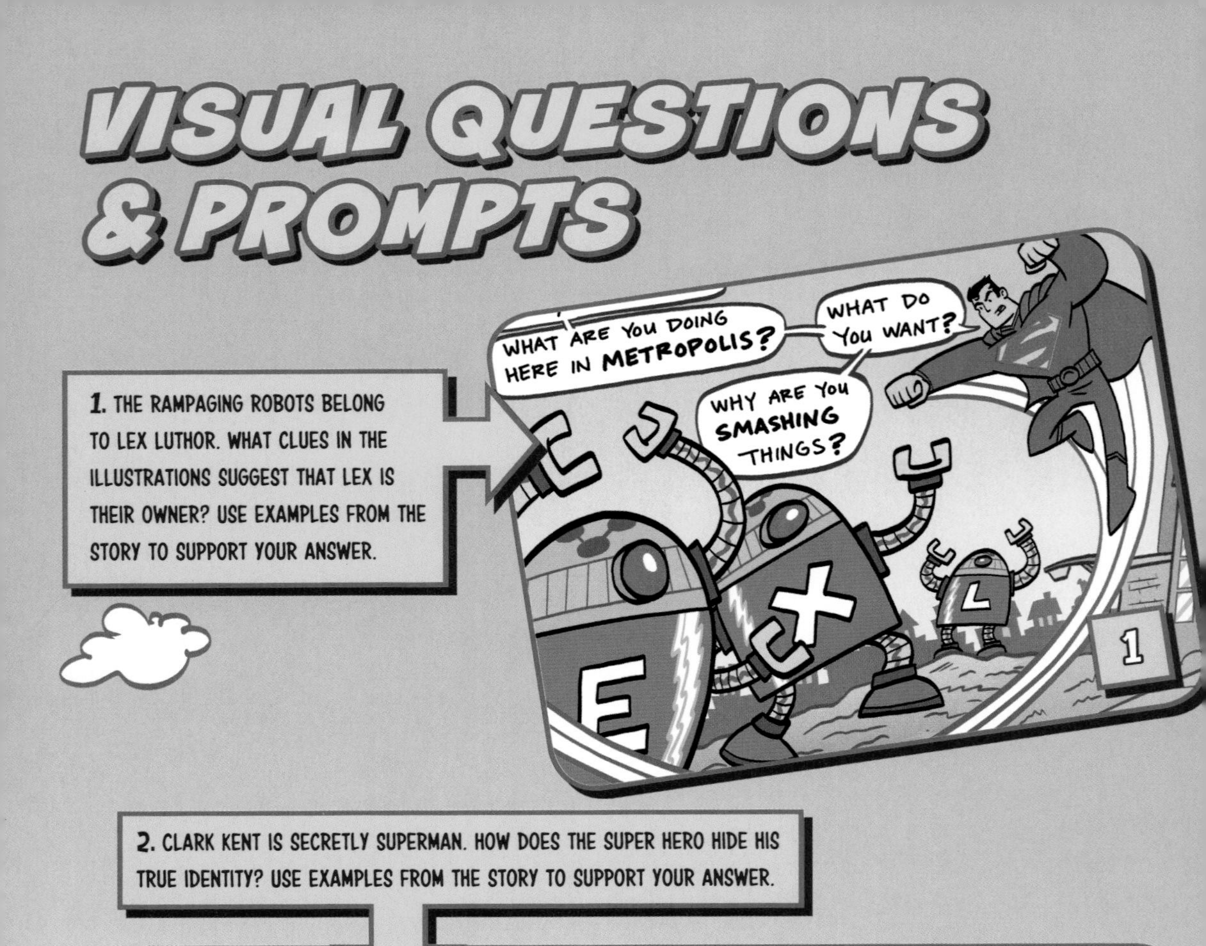
WHAT ARE YOU DOING HERE IN METROPOLIS?
WHAT DO YOU WANT?
WHY ARE YOU SMASHING THINGS?
1

2. CLARK KENT IS SECRETLY SUPERMAN. HOW DOES THE SUPER HERO HIDE HIS TRUE IDENTITY? USE EXAMPLES FROM THE STORY TO SUPPORT YOUR ANSWER.

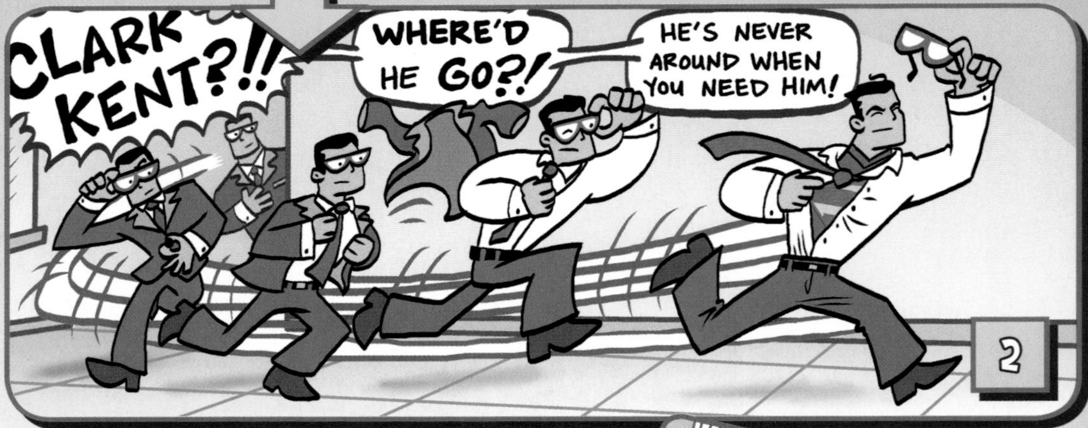
CLARK KENT?!!
WHERE'D HE GO?!
HE'S NEVER AROUND WHEN YOU NEED HIM!
2

3. SUPERMAN AND OTHER MEMBERS OF THE SUPER FAMILY HAVE MANY SUPERPOWERS, INCLUDING SUPER-STRENGTH, SUPER-SPEED, HEAT VISION, AND MORE. IF YOU COULD HAVE ANY SUPERPOWER, WHAT WOULD IT BE, AND WHY?

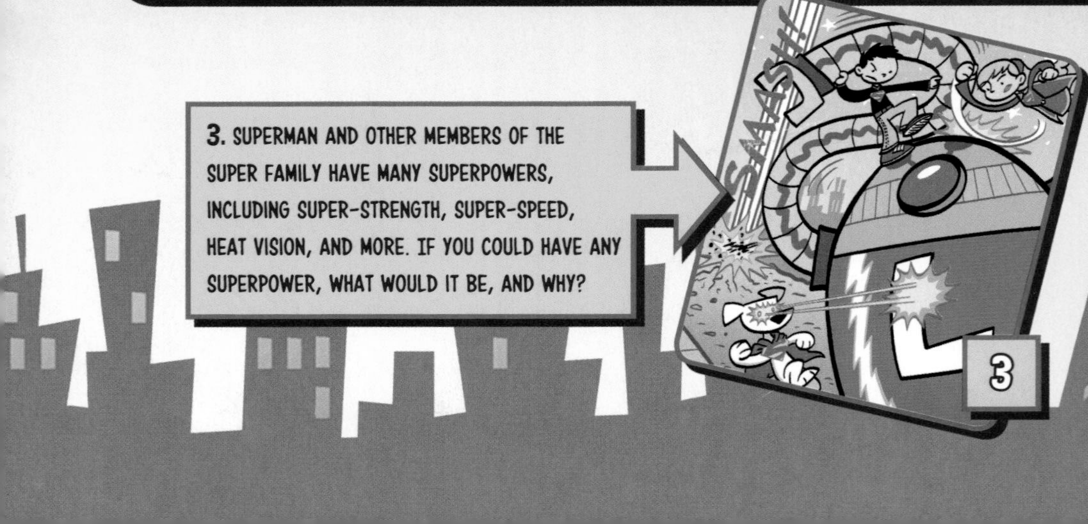
3

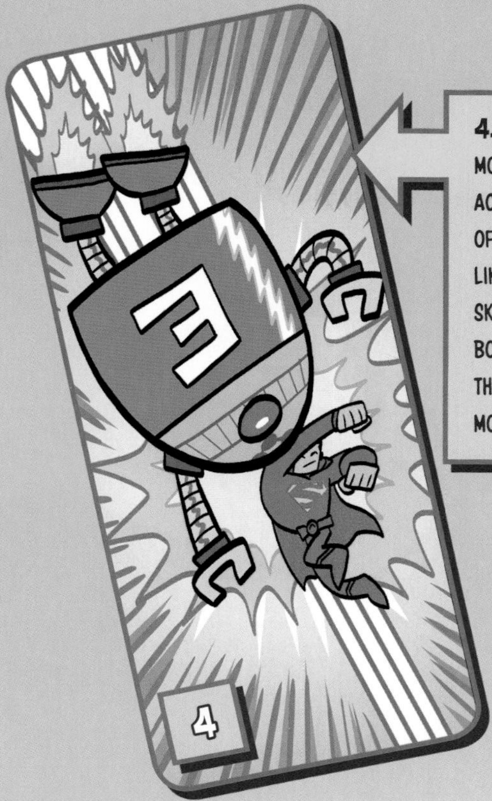
4

4. COMIC BOOK ILLUSTRATORS DRAW MOTION LINES (ALSO KNOWN AS ACTION LINES) TO SHOW MOVEMENT OF A CHARACTER OR AN OBJECT, LIKE SUPERMAN FLYING THROUGH THE SKY. FIND OTHER PANELS IN THIS BOOK WITH MOTION LINES. DO YOU THINK THEY MAKE THE ILLUSTRATIONS MORE EXCITING? WHY OR WHY NOT?

5. DESCRIBE WHAT IS HAPPENING IN THESE THREE PANELS FROM PAGE 14. HOW IS LEX LUTHOR ABLE TO SEE SUPERMAN ON HIS COMPUTER SCREEN? HOW DO YOU KNOW?

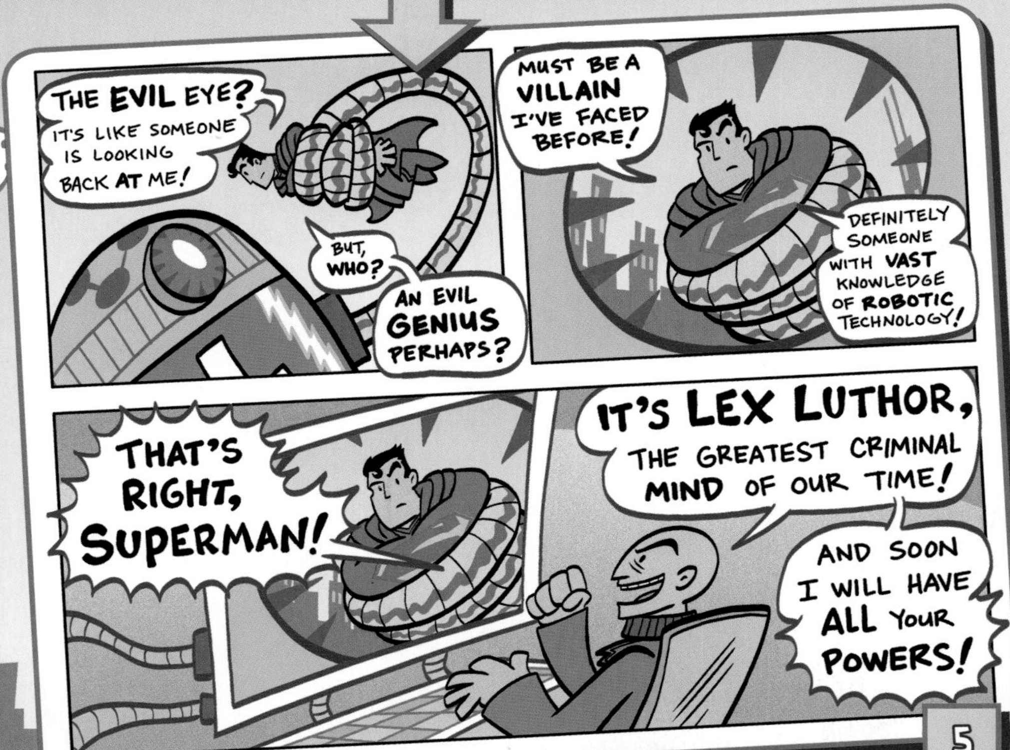
THE EVIL EYE? IT'S LIKE SOMEONE IS LOOKING BACK AT ME!
BUT, WHO?
AN EVIL GENIUS PERHAPS?
MUST BE A VILLAIN I'VE FACED BEFORE!
DEFINITELY SOMEONE WITH VAST KNOWLEDGE OF ROBOTIC TECHNOLOGY!
THAT'S RIGHT, SUPERMAN!
IT'S LEX LUTHOR, THE GREATEST CRIMINAL MIND OF OUR TIME!
AND SOON I WILL HAVE ALL YOUR POWERS!
5

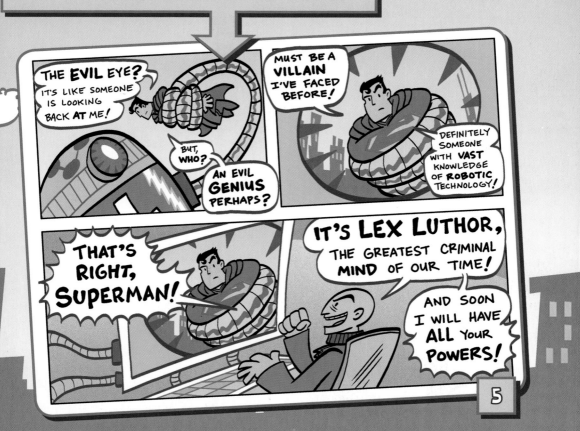

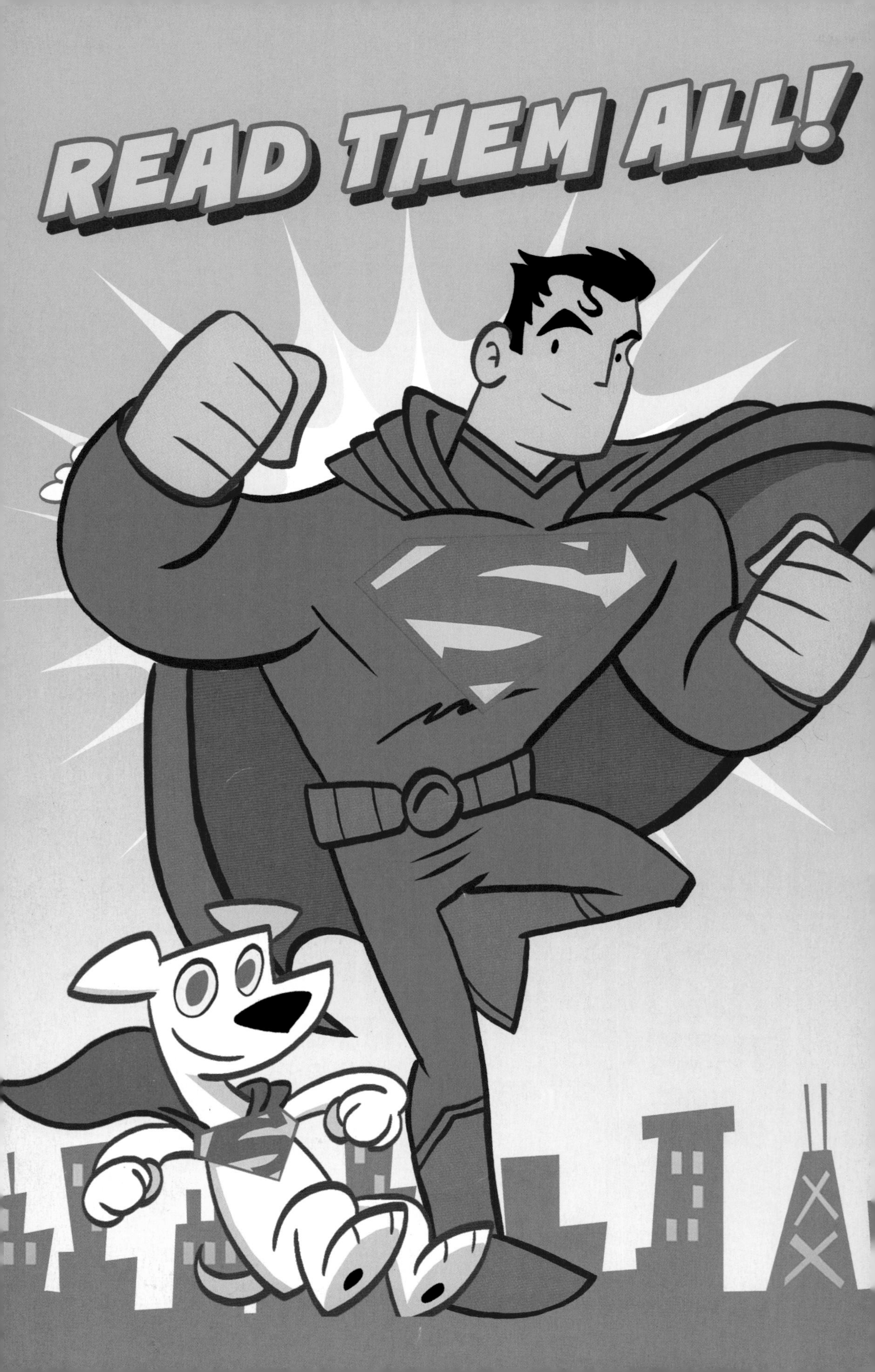
READ THEM ALL!

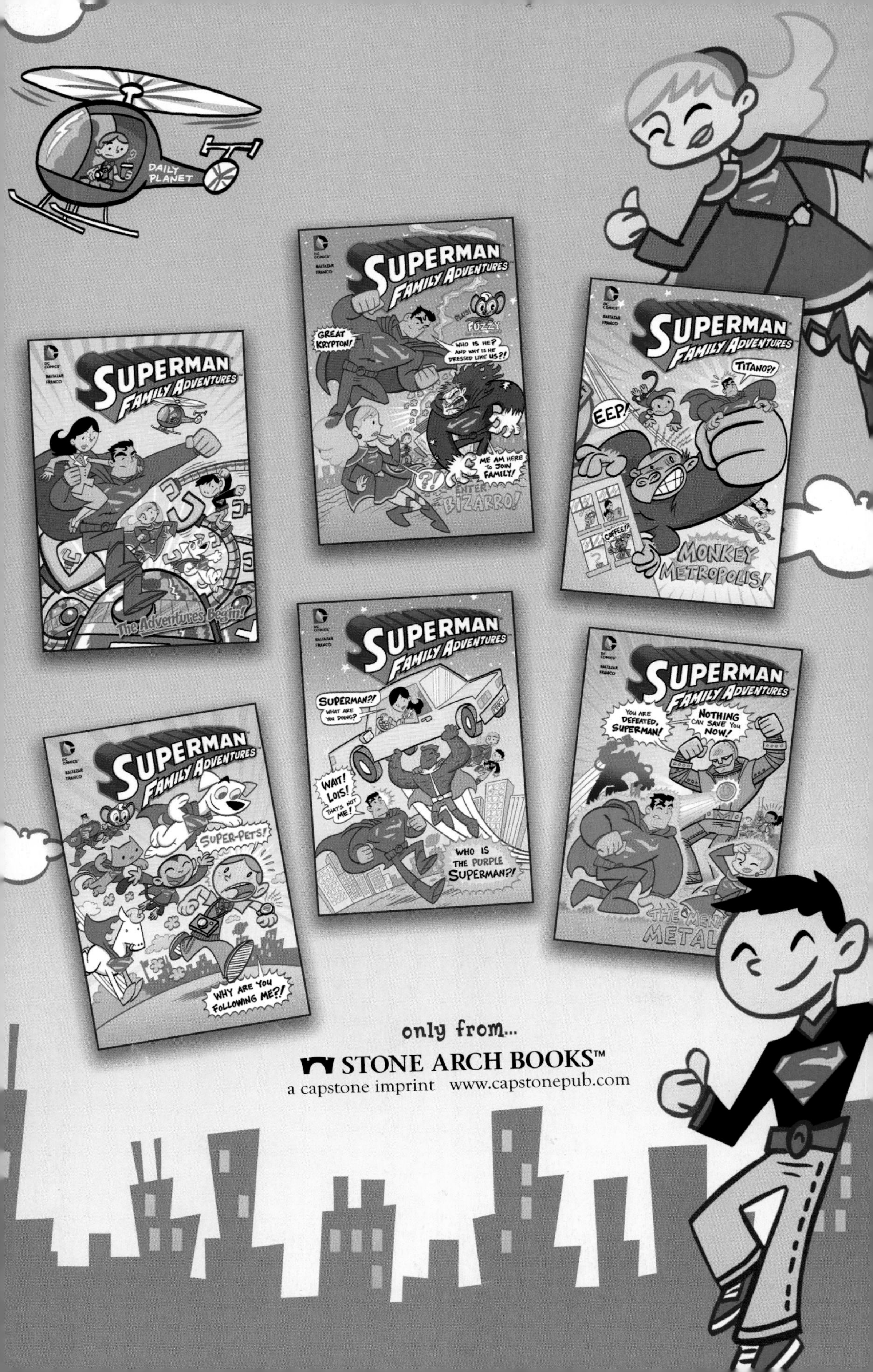
DAILY PLANET
SUPERMAN FAMILY ADVENTURES
BALTAZAR FRANCO
The Adventures Begin!
SUPERMAN FAMILY ADVENTURES
BALTAZAR FRANCO
GREAT KRYPTON!
WHO IS HE? AND WHY IS HE DRESSED LIKE US?!
FUZZY
ME AM HERE TO JOIN FAMILY!
?!
ENTER: BIZARRO!
SUPERMAN FAMILY ADVENTURES
BALTAZAR FRANCO
TITANO?!
EEP!
COFFEE!?
MONKEY METROPOLIS!
SUPERMAN FAMILY ADVENTURES
BALTAZAR FRANCO
SUPER-PETS!
WHY ARE YOU FOLLOWING ME?!
SUPERMAN FAMILY ADVENTURES
BALTAZAR FRANCO
SUPERMAN?! WHAT ARE YOU DOING?
WAIT! LOIS! THAT'S NOT ME!
WHO IS THE PURPLE SUPERMAN?!
SUPERMAN FAMILY ADVENTURES
BALTAZAR FRANCO
YOU ARE DEFEATED, SUPERMAN!
NOTHING CAN SAVE YOU NOW!

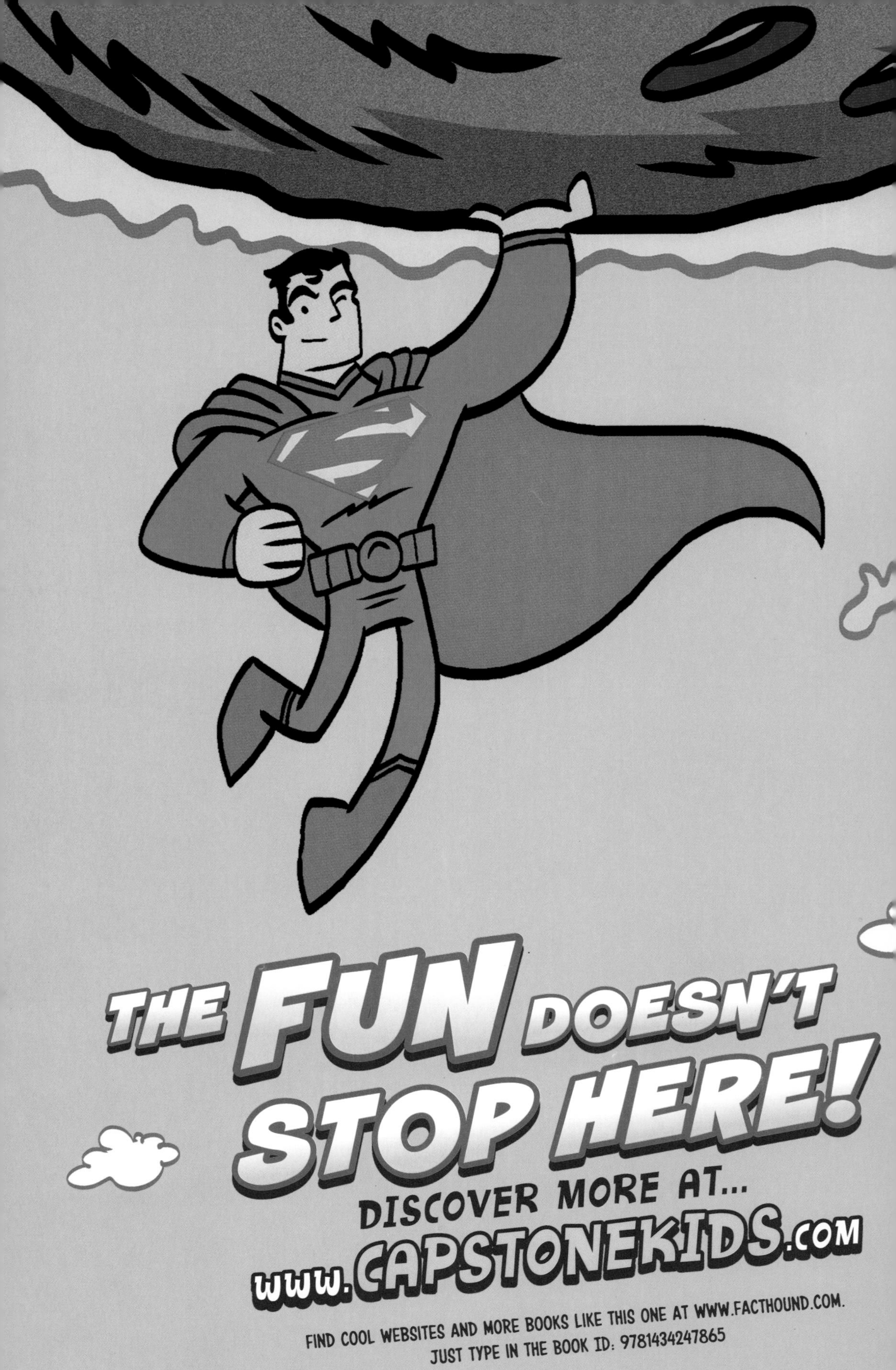